# THE WOLF AND HIS WIFE

WOLF #2

PENELOPE SKY

Hartwick Publishing

**The Wolf and His Wife**

Copyright © 2019 by Penelope Sky

All rights reserved.

No part of this book may be reproduced in any form or by any electronic or mechanical means, including information storage and retrieval systems, without written permission from the author, except for the use of brief quotations in a book review.

## CONTENTS

| | |
|---|---:|
| 1. Arwen | 1 |
| 2. Maverick | 15 |
| 3. Arwen | 37 |
| 4. Maverick | 49 |
| 5. Arwen | 63 |
| 6. Maverick | 79 |
| 7. Arwen | 97 |
| 8. Maverick | 107 |
| 9. Arwen | 119 |
| 10. Maverick | 135 |
| 11. Arwen | 141 |
| 12. Maverick | 153 |
| 13. Arwen | 171 |
| 14. Maverick | 187 |
| 15. Arwen | 205 |
| 16. Maverick | 219 |
| 17. Arwen | 233 |
| 18. Maverick | 247 |
| 19. Arwen | 259 |
| 20. Maverick | 267 |
| *Also by Penelope Sky* | 271 |

# 1

## ARWEN

We seemed to go back in time.

Maverick and I were strangers once more.

He went about his life and pretended I didn't exist. When he wasn't at the house, he was at work. Even late into the evenings, he seemed to stay at the office just so he wouldn't have to see me.

The man hated me.

Women came and went, replacing me in his bed.

I wasn't jealous of his lovers. I was jealous that I lost my wolf. Now, we were two strangers who never spoke to each other, who forgot about the connection we'd once had. We weren't even friends anymore.

It was all my fault.

Henry fell asleep, so I slipped out of bed and picked up my dress off the floor. The bedroom was dark, with the exception of the dim light from the street that entered through the window. After I finished a performance, I came here for affection...since I wasn't getting any at home.

As the soft fabric fell down my body and over my hips, I felt unsatisfied. The sex was good but not nearly as good as it'd been with Maverick. That man had hands that were meant to grab a woman. He had lips that knew how to kiss a woman. He had the perfect touch to make my toes curl, to make the air halt in my lungs as I writhed in ecstasy. I didn't usually compare lovers because they were all at about the same level. But now that I'd been with Maverick, I understood why so many women wanted to sleep in his bed.

Henry stirred when he heard me grab my heels. "Leaving?"

I'd been hoping to slip out without waking him. "Yes. I have an early morning tomorrow." That was a lie. I had nothing to do. My life revolved around the opera, and that took place in the evenings. I spent my days in a mansion without anyone to talk to.

He got out of bed and came up behind me. "You should stay anyway." His arms circled my waist, and he placed a kiss on my neck.

"No, I can't." I moved out of his reach and sat on the armchair so I could put my heels on.

He stood naked in front of me, his eyes filled with disappointment.

I ignored his nakedness and stood up again, grabbing my clutch off the table. "Goodnight, Henry." I headed to the door, my heels echoing off the hardwood floor.

He followed me, his large feet making a dull thump with his movements.

Before I could open the door, he grabbed me by the wrist and turned me around. I looked into his gaze, seeing the desire to yank me back and never let me go. The hair on the back of my neck stood on end, afraid he might actually do that.

He leaned in and kissed the corner of my mouth. "Come over tomorrow." He knew exactly when I was working because the production schedule was public information. So he always knew when I would be just down the street.

I didn't see this fling going anywhere. The sex wasn't good enough to keep having, and I found myself lying in the dark thinking about Maverick. I stressed about our relationship, how I would earn his trust again. He seemed to be the only thing on my mind…and Henry couldn't make me forget about it. The relationship didn't feel right, so it was time to move on. "This isn't working, Henry."

His eyes fell like I'd punched him in the stomach. They narrowed in offense and disappointment, like he hadn't seen my rejection coming. His fingers loosened on my elbow. "Why is that?"

I respected a man who had pride when he got dumped. The ones who begged and argued were clingy and annoying. He seemed to be the latter. "It doesn't matter. Take care, Henry." I walked out so I wouldn't have to see the irritated look on his face. I'd been down this road many times, ending a relationship with a man who wasn't ready to let go. Dante had been the first man to leave me—and it hurt. But that was how life worked… I didn't need to explain myself. Henry and I only had slept together a few times. It wasn't like it meant anything. I walked out the door and didn't look back.

"Arwen."

A conversation would just prolong the inevitable, and I wasn't in the mood for a lengthy discussion. It was late and I was tired. I wanted to sleep in my own bed and start a new day tomorrow. So I ignored him and kept walking.

---

I SAT ALONE at the breakfast table like I did every morning.

Maverick didn't join me anymore. He must take his meals in his office or somewhere else in the three-story mansion.

I poured cream into my coffee and watched the swirl develop. The table was covered with pastries, bread, and fruit. It was more food than a single person could eat, but Abigail insisted on serving me like I had the stomach of four grown men.

My eyes were focused on my coffee, so I didn't notice Maverick approach the table.

He pulled out a chair and took a seat.

I lifted my gaze and looked at him, nearly doing a double take when I saw his handsome countenance. It'd been a while since I'd seen him, and now I noticed his hair was a little shorter because he'd cut it. The shadow on his jawline was a little thicker as if he skipped the shave that morning. Unfortunately, there was still a hostile expression in his eyes, like he was just as annoyed with me as he was a week ago.

I didn't realize how much I'd missed him until we were finally in the same room together. My fingers rested on the handle of the mug as I stared at him, taking in his features like it'd been months since I'd last seen him.

He grabbed the pot and poured the coffee into his mug, his t-shirt gripping his physique nicely. He returned the pot then took a long drink, letting the caffeine wake him. He grabbed his silverware then turned his attention to his food.

I kept staring at him, watching him ignore me as he enjoyed his breakfast.

With his eyes downcast, he acted like I wasn't there at all.

"How are you?"

He lifted his gaze as he took his time chewing his smoked salmon, his eyes still filled with pieces of coal. "Ramon is dead."

I'd figured Caspian had butchered him a long time ago.

"My father tortured him then tossed his body into a river."

Ramon got what he deserved, but I did pity his family. When I rescued them, they knew it was the last time they would ever see him…and they knew what would happen to him before he finally died. "Did that make your father feel better?"

He took another bite, taking his time before he answered. "I doubt it."

"Have you talked to him?"

"No."

"Then how do you know he killed Ramon?"

"His men told me." He grabbed his coffee and took another drink.

"Did it make you feel better?" Did Maverick sleep better knowing the man who'd raped his mother was finally dead? Did it give him the closure he needed to move on?

He stared at me for a long time, debating the answer behind his eyes.

I waited for him to say something.

He never did. "How are things with your boyfriend?"

He would never ask a question like that because he didn't care. He was clearly being sarcastic, changing the subject so we wouldn't have to talk about his father anymore.

"He's not my boyfriend…and I ended things."

"Why?"

I shrugged. "Wasn't feeling anything."

"Did he fight for you like all the others?" he said, still sarcastic.

Maverick was the only man I'd ever slept with who didn't want more of me. He didn't become obsessed or possessive. He wasn't impressed with me, probably because he'd been with so many beautiful women. "He wasn't happy about it, but he'll get over it. What about you?"

"What about me?" he asked, still eating.

"I noticed a lot of women have been staying here."

"That's not unusual."

"Do you like any of them?"

He set down his fork and stared at me. "I don't *like* women. I fuck them and then move on."

He seemed to have moved on from me and didn't miss me at all. I missed the sex, but he seemed to get what he needed from other people. He was an amazing lover to me, but to him, I must be replaceable. "I'm really sorry about—"

"I don't want to talk about it ever again." He dismissed me and picked up his fork again. "Let's move on."

"Well…I hope we can be friends again. Because I really miss you." I stopped the emotion from entering my voice, but I could feel it crackle in my throat. Living in this mansion alone was a form of torture. I had no one to confide in, no one to share my life with. I missed watching movies with Maverick, missed talking in his office. He was my closest friend in the world, but now he was gone.

His eyes didn't react while he listened to my confession. "Friendships are built on trust. We don't have trust, so I don't see how we could ever be friends again."

"Maverick, I will always be loyal to you. I made a mistake, and I'm sorry for that—"

"But you said you wouldn't change your decision even if you could. That doesn't sound like an apology to me." His eyes flashed with hostility.

"Yes…but I would have done things differently."

He turned back to his food.

"I know you must care about me. If you didn't, you would have kicked me out. You changed your mind for a reason."

He kept eating.

I watched him, hoping for a reaction. "I understand you're mad at me right now, but I hope I can make it up to you somehow. If there's anything I can do, tell me. I'll do it. I want us to trust each other, to depend on each other. I want you to know that I respect and admire you…and I want things to be how they used to be."

He finished chewing his food before he raised his chin and looked at me. "I'm a simple man, Arwen. My requirements are small. Just don't fuck with me, and we won't have any problems. But you did fuck with me…and now I've got so much shit to deal with. I won't sweep that under the rug and forget about it."

"I understand…but maybe eventually you will."

His eyes were so cold. "The only reason I changed my mind was because I knew what would happen to you if I let you go. You wouldn't have lasted a week. Kamikaze probably would have found you first—and raped you."

My lungs deflated in fear.

"So, I let you stay…because you didn't deserve that. It doesn't mean I like you. It doesn't mean I forgive you. It doesn't mean I want anything to do with you. It just means that I didn't want you to be raped and murdered. Don't take it too personally." He pushed his plate away and grabbed his coffee.

"I do take it personally. You've been there for me in the past, and you're still here for me now. That means a lot to me. I want you to know I'll always be there for you…whatever you need."

He drank from his mug and ignored my offer. "I have a dinner party tomorrow night. You're coming with me."

The change in subject was so sudden, it nearly gave me whiplash. "What's this dinner party for?"

"It's one of my clients, a ridiculous social affair. I have to do them from time to time, and I have to take my wife along. Abigail picked out a dress for you. Just be ready by five."

Maybe spending time with Maverick could repair some of the damage. Maybe we could be close again, be friends again. "I have a performance tomorrow night...but I'll have my understudy take care of it. "

"You have a performance tonight as well?"

"Yes...you should come." Maverick had seen my show months ago, but we'd changed a few songs to keep it fresh. It would be nice to see him in the audience, to see him support my passion like a real husband.

He took another drink of his coffee then stood up.

"Do you think things will settle down with your father?" Was he still intent on killing me? Was he still enemies with Maverick? If we gave it enough time, would that problem subside?

He gripped the back of the chair as he looked at me, his eyes like two lasers. He had masculine knuckles, cords in his neck because his body was so tight. His dark hair was styled and ready for the day, making him deadly handsome. "He's my problem—not yours."

When the show ended, the curtains closed. Applause sounded from the auditorium, still making its way to my ears because it was so deafening. Once the lights were off my face, the temperature dropped by nearly ten degrees. I grabbed the sides of my dress and lifted the fabric as I headed backstage.

I exchanged hugs and words of congratulations with the cast and crew then made my way to my makeup station. My hair was pulled free from the pins then I dropped the enormous gown and changed into something less puffy for the drive home.

"Arwen." Henry's voice sounded nearby, desperate and clingy.

I turned around, surprised to see him standing right behind me. I was clear when I dumped him last night, and I didn't expect him to come to my show just to get my attention for another five minutes. He'd texted and called me a couple times last night, but I assumed he would give up by the next day.

Guess not.

"What are you doing here?" I demanded, immediately uncomfortable that he'd caught me off guard.

"I just wanted to talk to you. Last night, you just left—"

"No. Last night, I said I didn't want to see you anymore. It's nothing personal, Henry. It was just a fling, and I'm not interested in having that fling anymore. We weren't in a relationship to begin with. We only slept together a handful of times. You're making this into a bigger deal than it needs to be." Maybe I was jumping the gun, but I'd been in this position so many times that I was tired of having this same conversation over and over again.

"You think I'm just going to let you go without a fight?" he asked incredulously. "Come on, I'm not stupid."

"And I'm not yours to let go." I held up my left hand, where my large diamond reflected the lights from the mirror. "I'm married, Henry. This was never going to go anywhere, and you knew that. You need to back up and give me some space."

"I'm not asking you to marry me. I just don't see why we can't—"

"Because I don't want to. Our fling ran its course, and I'm ready for something new." Men never had to have this conversation with women. They had their one-night stands without explanation. But when the tables were turned, women weren't given the same opportunity.

His hand moved to my wrist. "Arwen, come on—"

"I said no."

He grabbed my wrist again.

"Grab my wife again, and that's the last thing you'll ever grab." Maverick's voice was more threatening than a loaded gun. His tone announced his hostility along with his promise of cruelty if his orders weren't obeyed. He emerged from nowhere, deadly in his suit and tie. With his hair perfectly styled and his brown eyes steaming, he moved beside me and stared Henry down. His hands rested in his pockets, and he didn't take a fighting stance because he didn't need to. His presence was terrifying enough.

Henry took a few seconds to react, to size up his opponent before realizing he had no possible chance against this formidable man. His fingers loosened, and he dropped my wrist, taking a step back.

Maverick came closer to my side, claiming his territory with his proximity. He slowly stepped closer to Henry, his eyes turning dominant like a wolf on the hunt. He stopped just inches from Henry, considerably taller. "Don't come near my wife again. I'll chop off both of your hands if you do." He kept his voice low so no one else could overhear the tense conversation taking place.

I was the one being rescued, but even I was scared.

Henry probably shit his pants. He finally stepped back and maneuvered around Maverick, leaving the backstage area and returning to the front of the stage. His eyes were downcast, like a submissive dog that had bowed to the alpha.

Maverick didn't turn to watch him leave. He directed his gaze on me next, his hands staying in his pockets. He'd managed to threaten a man without raising his voice or making a fist. And he did it so calmly, like the interaction nearly bored him.

I wasn't afraid Henry would hurt me, but I was irritated that my lover had become my stalker. Every time I wanted to slip away, he grabbed me tighter. It was a nuisance, like I didn't look over my shoulder already as it was. But my wolf came and scared off the monster…and I was grateful.

He watched me for a long time, his eyes trailing down my long hair and the tightness of my dress. He looked me over intimately, just the way he did when we were in bed together. The perusal lasted a short while before he looked me in the eye again, like the attraction never happened in the first place.

"Thank you."

"You weren't kidding. You really do have an effect on men."

Not on this man. "Why did you come tonight?"

"You asked me, remember?"

"But you didn't say anything."

He glanced at the people around us, the other cast members who had changed and were prepared to go home for the evening. He turned back to me, his shoulders wide in his suit. He looked beautiful naked, but he looked delicious in a suit. He had the perfect body that made his clothes fit him so well. "I rarely say anything."

"Yeah…I picked up on that. What did you think of the show?"

"I didn't pay attention to the show—only you. And you were amazing—as always."

This man rarely issued a compliment, so I took it straight to heart. "Thank you." Maybe my words got to him, made him miss our friendship the way I did. I couldn't think of any other explanation for why he was there, why he showed up to watch me perform songs he'd already heard.

"Let me walk you to your car." His arm circled my waist, and he guided me outside through the hallways, back to the place where we'd met the very first time. Down the steps and to the car, he guided me until we reached my black BMW, the new car he'd bought me since I'd given away my old one.

I pulled out my keys and hit the button to unlock the doors. "I'll see you at the house."

He opened the door for me, being a gentleman. "I'm going out. I'll see you tomorrow."

I stilled before I lowered myself into the front seat, suddenly disappointed that Maverick would be visiting a bar to find a woman to take home. He'd stopped by my show on the way since he was in the city anyway. Why did I expect anything different? "Alright…be safe."

"Sheep, I'm always safe."

## 2

## MAVERICK

I brought the wineglass to my lips and took a drink, noting the flavors of berries, oak, and even age. My fingers gripped the stem of the glass as I let the smoothness roll across my tongue, savoring the richness that had been perfectly fermented.

Tony stood beside me, his eyes moving past my frame as he watched something on the other side of the room. "I never congratulated you on your wedding. It's only been a few months, so you must be in the honeymoon stage."

Far from it. "Thank you."

He continued to stare.

I followed his gaze and watched where it landed. Arwen stood in a black cocktail dress, skintight and backless, with five-inch heels that made her height more compatible with mine. With a glass of wine in her hand, she talked to some of the guys who had cornered her, becoming a highlight of the evening since most people recognized her from the opera.

Tony was married, but he didn't seem to care if his wife noticed the subject of his obsession. "You lucked out, Maverick. She's one hell of a beauty."

She turned heads everywhere she went. I noticed it anytime we were in public together. Men couldn't control themselves and eye-fucked her like their fantasy might be reality someday. "Thank you."

"How did you meet?"

I went with the truth. "At the opera. She performed, and I went backstage to talk to her."

"And the rest is history?" he asked.

I swirled my wine. "Something like that."

"The sex good?"

I lowered my glass and stared at him, finding the question offensive. I was used to men saying inappropriate things about my wife's legs and her gorgeous ass, but I let them slide because her sexiness was impossible to ignore. But I didn't appreciate a question so intimate. I never talked about my lovers like that, not with Kent or anyone else. "How's the sex with your wife?"

When he grew uncomfortable at the question, I'd made my point.

Tom walked up to me, wearing a dark blue suit with a black tie. Everyone in the room was an affluent member of society, the rich and aristocratic of Italy. They were business owners, models, and designers. I put up with the boredom because they were excellent connections to have for business purposes. He reached me and gripped me by the shoulder. "We've been trying to convince your wife to sing us a song. She's too shy, so how about you give her a nudge?"

Like that woman ever listened to me. "She's stubborn."

"You're stubborn too, so you're perfect for the job." He clapped me on the back then guided me across the room.

Arwen was surrounded by admirers, both men and women, trying to get her to serenade everyone in the room. Despite her talent, she was unusually humble about it. It was something she never talked about with me, only if I asked. Her eyes settled on me when I came close, and I saw the gentle look of affection she always gave whenever I was concerned. She'd despised me when we first met, but now she turned to me the way she used to turn to her father. "I know why they've sent you…"

I came close to her, circling my arm around her waist and holding her close. I acted like her husband, not just to put on a show, but so the guys would stop eye-fucking her right in front of me. She didn't mean anything to me, but she was still mine. I didn't like it when people eyed my things. "Just a song."

"I don't know…so many people here."

"Not more than an entire auditorium."

"But I don't know these people…"

"You don't know anyone at the theater either."

She opened her mouth to argue once more.

"Sheep, just do it."

She closed her mouth at the use of her nickname, her eyes softening at the affection.

"I scared off your admirer. You owe me."

"I owe you for a lot more than that, Maverick." Her arm rested on mine as her hand gripped my bicep. Her affection for me was peculiar because she seemed to admire me and respect me, but all she wanted was my friendship. She wanted to be my lover sometimes, but she didn't want to be the only woman in my life. It was a strange relationship, so deep and so shallow at the same time.

"Then sing." My hand released her waist, and I stepped away, leaving her alone in front of the fireplace while everyone gathered around to hear those amazing pipes release a beautiful song. Without accompanying instruments, it would be a song from her voice alone—but it would still be perfect.

She gave a nervous smile and brought her fingertips together before she finally opened her mouth to sing. Without even warming up, she managed to produce the perfect notes through no effort, creating a song that mesmerized everyone—including me.

Tony stood beside me, not taking a single drink from his glass through the entire performance. No one else moved an inch. They hardly even breathed. They were all equally entranced by the music she created, by the vivid picture she painted with just her voice. Not a single person cared about anything else at that moment.

At the end of her song, her voice reached so high, it resonated with the particles in the air, made the entire room shift with the energy. Empty glasses on the table shattered when she hit the highest note, exploding because of her power.

Then she ended the song.

Everyone looked around at the destroyed glasses then applauded, even more impressed with her talent at such a more intimate level than in an auditorium.

I was the only one who didn't clap—because I wasn't surprised.

---

She sat beside me at the table, cutting her fork into her cheesecake and bringing a taste to her lips. "Damn...this is good."

My arm rested across the back of her chair, keeping the dogs away from my wife. Every man in that room was an acquaintance I socialized with on a regular basis, but they couldn't control themselves around Arwen. They turned into horny teenagers who were obsessed with the most beautiful girl in school. They eyed me with envy, wishing she were theirs instead of mine.

I'd never thought she could be instrumental in business. That night, I got more invitations for collaborations than I'd ever had. Restaurant owners asked for bigger shipments of my product, and other acquaintances asked for aged wheels for their dinner parties. They came flooding to me—all because of the woman I married.

But I would never tell her that.

She cut into her cheesecake again and took another bite.

"Maverick, you have to try this…" She wiped the fork down her tongue then closed her eyes as she savored it. "I've never had cheesecake this good in my entire life."

When I looked up, I saw a few men watching her, getting off on the way she got off on her dessert.

Fuck, these men couldn't keep it in their pants.

"I'm good." I grabbed her fork and put it down, cutting her off from her affair with her dessert. "That's enough."

"Uh, I'll eat all that I want." She grabbed her fork again. "I don't care if my hips get bigger."

"That's not what I'm worried about." I grabbed the fork again and put it down. "You're making every man in here hard as a rock." That included me. "Now, if you can't stop eating like a porn star, then you can't eat."

"What?" she asked, keeping her voice low. "You're being ridiculous."

"No, I'm not. Do as I say. Don't make me ask you again."

Normally, she would tell me off or smear the dessert across my face, but since we were surrounded by people, she kept her mouth shut. She also probably played nice since she'd fucked up so badly. She owed me—and she knew it.

She picked up the fork and kept eating, this time behaving like a normal person. She cut down the sexiness and did her best to blend in with everyone else.

Good.

"Should we offer to pay for the glasses I broke?"

"No. That would be offensive."

"How so?"

"Because that implies he can't pay to replace them. You know how rich people are."

"I guess it's been a while now…" She turned her gaze back to her cheesecake and took another bite. "I've got a few hundred bucks in my account, so I guess the cost of a single glass is a big deal to me."

"You're my wife—which means you have billions in your account."

She kept eating and ignored what I said. She still hadn't used any of the money I put in her account. She lived off her meager checks from the opera to buy her clothes and accessories.

I was annoyed with her stubbornness, but I also respected it. She valued her independence and didn't want to spend my money on superficial stuff she didn't need. She was a simple person now.

"People here seem to admire you." She set down her fork and looked at me, guests mingling around us as the night drew to a close.

"You're confusing admiration for respect."

"Or maybe they're the same thing."

They weren't in my book. I pulled back my sleeve and checked the time. It was getting late, almost eleven. We still had a long drive back to the house. "We should get going."

"I wish I could take this cheesecake home."

"I can have Abigail bake an entire round for you."

"No, that'd be a terrible idea."

"Why?"

"Because I'd eat it all."

---

I LOOSENED my tie once we were in the car and popped open the first button. We were in my Bugatti, so I sped out of the city and into the countryside, pushing the car to a hundred and eighty kilometers per hour.

None of the cops would dare to pull me over.

She looked out the window from the passenger seat, her dress riding up on her thighs because it was so short. She would normally tug it down, but since it was just the two of us, she let it be.

I tried not to stare.

She had been the most beautiful woman in that room tonight, and that gave me a great sense of pride. She was a trophy I owned, a piece of real estate everyone wanted. Having a wife used to be a pain, but she'd become useful. At least it helped my image...and my business.

And I couldn't help but agree with everyone else... she was exceptional.

Her hair was in curls, her makeup was dark, and she'd painted her lips the sexiest color, a deep red that almost looked burgundy. Diamond earrings sat in her lobes, and that dress fit her perfect body in the sexiest way.

We didn't talk during the drive home, and we didn't have music on either. It was just silence.

My eyes were on the road when I felt her hand reach for my thigh. Her fingers gently dug into my slacks, her sharp nails reminding me of the way she'd cut my back in the past. After the squeeze, her fingers continued to rest there, subtly inviting me to her bed tonight.

It was tempting.

I turned to her and saw the way she looked at me, the way her mascara made her eyelashes look so thick. They made her eyes stand out so beautifully, especially when she wore dark colors that enhanced their vibrancy. Her lips were delectable in that shade, the perfect color to smear against my base after as she gave me a deep kiss.

I eye-fucked her the way everyone else had that evening.

I forced my gaze back on the road so we wouldn't crash, slightly distracted by the way her fingers kept digging into me. Her hand moved higher until she found exactly what she was looking for—my hard dick.

We arrived at the house minutes later, tensions running high. She wanted me, and with the way she looked tonight, I wanted her too.

But I was still pissed about the stunt she'd pulled. My father was now my enemy, and I had to watch my back every second of the day because I never knew when he would strike. That made me push her away, made me wish I didn't find her attractive at that moment.

We went into the house and walked to the second floor, where I would drop her off before continuing on my way to my bedroom on the next landing. I wanted to dismiss her and turn away, but her fingers snaked into mine until they were locked together.

It reminded me of the way she'd gripped my hand at the funeral, how she conveyed so much emotion in that simple embrace. She'd squeezed our fingers together, tears streaking down her face. She'd told me I was her rock...the only man she could count on.

It always turned me on when she needed me. And she needed me now.

She faced me, her hand still held in mine. In those heels, she was much taller than usual, her back dipping at a beautiful angle to make her ass stick out even farther. She moved into me, her fingers releasing from mine so she could push her hands up my chest. Slowly, her fingers dug under my jacket until she pushed it off my shoulders, leaving me in just my collared shirt. She wanted me—and she didn't want there to be any misunderstanding.

She stepped closer to my chest and pressed her lips to mine, her eyes still open as she looked at me. Her lips landed softly, like a teardrop on a pillow. She inhaled the second she felt my mouth, like the chemistry was just as strong as ever. Her eyes closed, and her hand slid into my hair as she brought me in for a passionate kiss.

I let her pull me, let her have me. My lips moved with hers, and the taste of cheesecake was impossible to ignore. I could taste the sweetness as it combined with her desire, making it the best thing I'd ever tasted. My hands moved to her ass, and I bent my neck down as she continued to pull me into her.

She moaned into my mouth.

My hands gripped her ass under her dress, feeling the soft skin of her cheeks as well as the lace of her thong.

"Fuck me." She spoke against my mouth, enticing me with her touch. Her demand came out heavy, the words weighed down with so much desire. She pulled off the order so well, making it sexy enough for a fantasy.

I knew every man in that room tonight wished he were me right now.

But that wasn't enough to make me drop my pants. That wasn't enough to invite her into my bed for the night. It didn't matter how sexy her legs were, how good of a kisser she was. She'd crossed me—and I still wasn't over it.

I ended the kiss and pulled back. "Goodnight, Sheep."

She stood there with parted lips, wounded by the way I'd rejected her. Disbelief was in her gaze, as if she couldn't believe I'd turned her down—again. Desire was still in her eyes, like she would take me if I changed my mind. "Maverick—"

"I'm still pissed at you." As her husband, I would always protect her from clingy assholes who didn't understand the meaning of no. I would defend her from the sexist comments men couldn't hold back. I would buy her a new car when she gave her old one away. But I wouldn't turn the other cheek when she betrayed what I cared about most —trust.

"It's just sex…"

Any other guy would have the same thought. It didn't matter

if she stabbed me in the back; she was still so damn fuckable. It was just meaningless sex, sweaty and dirty fucking. It shouldn't matter to me. But for whatever reason, it did. "I get sex all the time, so I don't need this." I turned around and headed up the stairs, adding to the harsh words I said to her as I blew her off. "I don't need you."

---

I DIDN'T SEE Arwen the next day.

I got up early, worked out, and then went to the office. I kept busy, working on orders and making sure my important clients got exactly what they wanted. Some of them spent ten thousand dollars on a single wheel of cheese because it'd been aged for almost two decades. Those had to be handled with the highest care.

At the end of the day, I sat in my office and looked out the window, watching the sun go down. It was the end of summer, so the sun set a little earlier than usual. I liked to watch the colors change from blue to pink and purple. With a glass of scotch in my hand, I found it the most relaxing part of my day.

When night had completely fallen, I left my office and drove back to the house. I wasn't necessarily avoiding Arwen, but I didn't look forward to seeing her. I hadn't blown her off because I was uncomfortable with her reaction. I just didn't feel like talking about it.

Abigail had dinner waiting for me downstairs, so I ate before I went up to the third floor. The second I was at the top of the stairs, I heard the most beautiful voice.

"Seasons change, plants come back to life, but you're gone forever…and I've already said goodbye." Piano keys were being played lightly by master fingertips. The music was soft and quiet, completely opposite from the burst of song she produced in the auditorium. This was intimate and sexy, just her and the piano.

I walked down the hallway, passing the door where the piano stood behind the closed door.

"My heart withers with broken strings, while you've gotten your wings…"

I stopped outside the door, listening to the beautiful way she hit her notes without even trying. She wasn't just an excellent singer, but a master of her craft. I didn't recognize the song, and I wondered if she'd written it herself…because it reminded me of her father.

I kept going, the sound of her voice growing quieter as I entered my bedroom. Even when I shut the door behind me, I could still hear her voice, hear the melancholy she conveyed so well.

Instead of hopping in the shower or pouring myself a drink after the long day I'd had, I continued to stand there and listen, my ears straining to hear the beautiful lyrics that resonated with my soul.

Just as always happened when she sang in front of everyone at the party, I was hard. I was hard anytime I heard her sing, both times I'd watched her sing at the opera. Something about her voice pulled at my desire. Now my dick didn't think twice before expanding in my pants. All I needed was the melody of her voice, and I was ready to go.

Ready to fuck.

I tried to ignore the lovely music, but I couldn't. I hummed to myself as the song instantly got stuck in my head. Images of her on the piano flooded my mind, her legs open as I thrust into her, our tangled bodies playing the keys with our passion.

I rejected her last night—but now I wanted her more than ever.

I left my bedroom and returned down the hallway, approaching the drawing room where the grand piano stood in the corner. I'd never played the instrument myself, nor did I have a particular love of music. It was simply an elegant piece to decorate this mansion.

I cracked the door and peered inside. Her chin was down and her eyes were focused on the keys, so absorbed in her music that she didn't even notice me. Her lithe fingers moved across the keyboard, gently stroking the black keys then the white. She wasn't reading music, playing something from memory.

I inched farther into the room, seeing the way a few strands had come loose from her bun. They hung in front of her face, the dark locks matching the color of the piano. She was in a halter top dress, deep blue and short. Her rounded shoulders looked elegant as she held herself with perfect poise. She was a musician practicing her craft, a professional that understood the notes and keys better than most people.

I grew more mesmerized by the second, entranced by her beautiful mouth and the breathtaking sounds she made. Now I was a dog just like the rest of the guys, trapped under her gorgeous spell.

I slowly approached the piano, the volume of the music growing louder. When my hand rested on the surface of the instrument, she finally realized she wasn't alone.

Her slender fingers stopped playing the keys, the music coming to a halt and making the silence sound so ugly. With embarrassment in her eyes, she lifted her gaze and looked at me, as if she'd been discovered doing something wrong—not something magical. "Jesus...you scared me."

I stood at the piano and watched her, seeing the beautiful glow in her eyes fade away as her concentration was broken.

She pulled her hands away from the keys and stood up.

"Keep playing."

She held her stance as she stared at me, considering what I'd said. Then she lowered herself back down but didn't return her hands to the keys. Arwen was never self-conscious about anything, even getting rejected by a man. But knowing I'd been watching her this entire time clearly unnerved her. It was the only time I'd ever seen her so unsure of herself. "I think I'm done anyway..."

I took a seat on the couch facing the piano, watching her and hoping she would change her mind.

The silence continued—because she was so damn stubborn.

"Did you write that song?"

She turned to me, slightly horrified I'd heard it. "Yeah..."

"It was beautiful."

She looked down again, dismissing my comment.

"You know I don't lie, Sheep. If I say something, I mean it." I wouldn't inflate her damaged ego with false praise. If she'd sucked, I would have stormed into the room and told her to quiet down. I wouldn't be sitting there now, staring at her with new eyes, if I didn't mean my words.

She lifted her gaze again.

"You write a lot of your own music?"

"All the time."

"I never knew that." I'd never asked her about her musical talents. I'd never really been interested in her, not the way most men were. To everyone else, she was beautiful, talented, and fascinating. I took her for granted. "Was that song about your father?"

Her eyes immediately filled with emotion, like I'd pressed an invisible button that made her lose her sanity. It was a touchy subject for her, losing the only man who ever loved her. "Yes..." She sniffed then looked at the piano again, like it was her safe place.

"I liked it."

She stared at the keys for a long time before she stood up. She brushed her hands over her dress and smoothed it out before she stepped toward the couch. "I didn't think you could hear me."

"I like hearing you." The second I heard the music, it washed my stress away. It made my muscles relax, made my body hum to life. It made me aroused, made me want to hear music from her lips while I was inside her.

She stopped and stared at me for a moment, like those

words meant something to her. But she turned her head and stepped away, dismissing them altogether.

My hand grabbed her wrist, and I steadied her.

She still didn't look at me.

I slowly tugged on her arm, pulling her in my direction so she would come into my lap. But I didn't pull on her so hard that she didn't have a choice. She could either move with my suggestion, or she could move away altogether and walk out.

She let me pull her. Closer and closer she came, her knees hitting mine once she was close to me.

My hands grabbed her hips, and I pulled her onto my lap, making her legs straddle my hips so she was directly on top of me. Her dress rose up her thighs, and I took it a step further and pulled it above her hips. Last night, my desire couldn't outweigh my rage, but right now, I wanted this woman. The music had stopped, but I was still under her spell, still hypnotized by her voice.

I rested my neck against the back of the chair and looked up at her, my hands feeling her curves. I started at the bottom of her ass, touched the curve of her cheeks, then slid into the valley of her back. Farther up I went, taking the dress with me. I slowly pulled it over her head and tossed it onto the couch.

Her perfect and perky tits were right in my face, so round and firm with nipples made for sucking. They were pale but flushed with color as her heart brought blood to the surface of her skin. Little bumps erupted across the surface, showing her arousal as well as her discomfort.

I took a moment to look at her, to stare at this perfect

woman on my lap. In just her panties, she was a wet dream. She was the sexiest woman I'd ever been with, possessing the kind of beauty that would make other girls spiteful. My hand reached up and yanked the tie from her hair, letting the strands fall across her shoulders. Still slightly curled from last night, they reached the bottom of her tits, the perfect length.

My hands cupped her ass, and I brought her close to my chest, making her face hover over mine. My big hands squeezed her beautiful globes, kneading them with my long fingers. I'd slept alone last night, and my dick was pissed. Now he was harder than he'd been the night before, horny and anxious.

Her hand slid into my hair, and she looked me in the eye as she held herself over me. Her lips descended slowly, her eyes watching my reaction as she combined our mouths together. The landing was perfect, making both of us breathe hard at the connection. My hands squeezed her ass again, and she pulled my hair until it tugged on my scalp.

Like every other time we'd kissed, it was so good. With the perfect ratio of lips to tongue, we were in sync anytime our bodies combined together. Sometimes women kissed too quickly and rushed to the passionate embraces when there hadn't been time for it to build up. But Arwen knew exactly how to kiss a man, to make my lips yearn for hers.

My dick pressed against my zipper as it fought to get closer to her, slip inside her perfect slit. My body ached for hers. My fingers trembled at the prospect of feeling her.

I wanted to fuck my wife so damn hard.

She pulled my shirt over my head then worked the top of

my jeans to get them undone. Without taking her lips off mine, she tugged them off my hips and far enough down so my cock could come free. Her hands found him and gently stroked him, her thumb swiping across the lube that formed at the tip of my crown.

One of my hands slid into her hair, and I gripped her tit at the same time, my dick throbbing in her hands. Nothing would stop me from having this woman now. A meteorite could strike the earth, but it wouldn't slow me down.

My hand reached into my front pocket, and I pulled out a condom. With a quick tear, I got it free and rolled it down to my base, securing it before I made the journey into her tight cunt. I grabbed her hip and pulled her down, forcing her to sink slowly until my enormous dick was inside her.

She moaned when she felt me, her eyes fading into pure lust. She wanted me with the same desire as last night, like she needed me to get the climax she craved. Her arms circled my neck, and she kissed me as she arched her back and moved up and down, slowly pushing her body down my length until her lips kissed my balls. Over and over, she repeated the same movements, pushing my length deep inside her and making her shiver.

Fuck, my wife was good in bed.

My hands returned to her luscious ass, and I guided her movements, my balls aching because I couldn't wait to fill the tip of the condom. Before I even approached the finish line, I could feel the load deep in my shaft, feel the amount of arousal I was about to spill out.

Things got hot and heavy quickly. She breathed hard against my mouth as she worked her body to fuck me. She held on to the back of my neck and moaned loudly, grinding her clit against my body to give her that extra push she needed to turn into a writhing puddle of ecstasy.

I watched her face, seeing her in a whole new way. She was so beautiful when she was getting fucked, her cheeks red and her lips anxious. Sometimes she bit her bottom lip when my cock felt particularly good, when it was hitting the perfect spot to make her hips buck on their own. Her nails clawed at me, and sometimes a pained moan escaped her lips, like she couldn't tolerate the pleasure. "Wolf...I'm gonna come so hard." Her nails started to slice me as she lost her mind, as the pleasure exploded inside her and made her writhe.

My hands gripped her ass and guided her up and down, feeling the tightness surround my dick once her pussy clenched around me like an iron fist. I'd fucked this cunt enough times to understand its subtleties, the way it tightened before it released. I could feel her pleasure through our combined bodies, feel how good she felt.

Tears sprung to her eyes, and she moaned in my face, her nipples sharp like two knives. "Yes...yes." Her voice trembled with her release, the moisture in her eyes welling up until two tears streaked down her cheeks.

Damn, she came hard.

Her hips stopped pounding into me as she slowed down, as the pleasure faded from her fingertips and toes. She caught her breath as she latched on to me, still enjoying the aftershocks of goodness in her veins.

The tears were so sexy to me that I came with a grunt, turned on by her emotional response to my dick. Every woman had a different reaction to a climax, but criers were rare. Arwen released tears like it was the biggest event of her life, the biggest climax she'd ever had. Seeing my wife in tears turned me on, made me release a load before I could control it.

She lowered her body until I was completely inside her, letting me come with my balls against her ass. "Give it to me..." Her palms rested against my chest as she looked me in the eye, watching me get off on her like it turned her on the way it turned me on.

I felt my dick shiver as I delivered my load, as I filled the tip of the condom to maximum capacity. My fingers dug into her ass as I finished, as my hips gave a final buck. The climax was enough to make all my muscles cramp with tightness. When I finished, I kept her on my lap, wanting to be inside her as my dick slowly softened.

I looked at her face, admiring the same arousal in her eyes that I knew was in mine. She was never more beautiful than when she'd been satisfied. A woman like that should be fulfilled every single day of her life. I'd always thought if I took a wife, I would always be the best sex she ever had.

And I had a feeling that was true with Arwen.

## 3

## ARWEN

Naked and wrapped in the sheets, I lay beside Maverick. My arm was draped over his waist, and my leg was tucked in between his. I wasn't sure how we made it from the drawing room into his enormous bed. A faint memory of him carrying me across the hall came to mind, his powerful arms supporting my body as he placed me on the cloud of sheets.

My eyes opened, and his body came into view, just as tight in the morning as it was in the evening. His tanned skin had beautiful grooves of hard muscle, gorgeous cuts I liked to dip my fingers into. Sleep was still heavy in my gaze and I was too tired to move, so I lay there and stared at this beautiful man.

As I remembered last night, I could feel the memory of tears in my eyes. I remembered the way they had watered when he made me come, more than I ever had before. He was a much better lover than Henry had ever been, better than any man in my past. He was so confident in his gaze, sexy in his kiss, and dominant in his grasp. He touched me the way a man should touch a woman, full of spark.

I wanted to stay there forever.

Maverick was the foundation my life was built on. He was my closest friend, my protector, and my lover. All of those attributes combined together and solidified what he really was—my husband.

My husband.

It had a nice ring to it.

He gently reached for the phone on his nightstand and tried not to disturb me as he moved, thinking I was still asleep. He scrolled through the list of emails waiting for him, all of them pertaining to the business he ran right on his property. He skimmed over most of them, opening a couple but not composing a reply.

I wanted to stay still so I wouldn't have to leave.

He grew impatient and started to move out of my embrace.

My fingers immediately tightened against his frame, keeping him in place because I didn't want him to slip away just yet. He probably had to complete his workout before heading to the office, but I wasn't ready to let him go.

He sat up and looked down at me, his sleepy gaze studying me beside him. His hair was a mess from the way I'd played with it all night long, and that only complimented his sexy look. His brown eyes looked into mine but he didn't say a word, his chin becoming dark with the shadow of his beard.

My hand slid into his dark hair, and I pulled him close to me, getting that large body on top of mine. I pulled him gently, then tugged harder, urging him to smother me into the mattress with his size, suffocate me with his smell. "I want you..." With my lips pressed close to his, I whispered my desires, admitted my neediness. My best nights of sleep happened in this bed, with my wolf beside me. It was the safest place in the world, the one place where no one could ever touch me.

He moved between my legs as he held himself on top of me, his powerful arms flexing as he held up his frame packed with muscle. His thighs kept mine wide apart, and he brushed his lips over mine, teasing me.

My fingers fisted his hair, and I brought his lips to mine, kissing him just as passionately as I did last night. He'd found me in my most vulnerable state, my fingers striking the keys of the grand piano. I'd sung under my breath, whispered a tune from my weeping heart. My walls were down, and I was exposed for what I was—a heartbroken woman. He accepted me that way, admired me that way.

He kissed me so good, caressed my lips like I was the only woman he ever wanted to kiss. Heated breaths fell across my lips, and a sensual tongue entered my mouth. Everything he did was sexy, from the way he breathed to the way he touched me. When he was on top of me like this, it was the sexiest thing in the world, to be pinned down by this animal with nowhere to run.

Not that I wanted to go anywhere.

When my nails started to slice his back in longing, he pulled away and grabbed a condom from his drawer. With expertise, he ripped open the packet and secured it over his base, leaving a large tip because he expected to produce a big load. Then he slipped inside me, stretching me like he'd never taken me before. Slowly he sank, inch by inch, until his balls tapped against my ass.

How could I take another man to bed when Maverick was the best?

When every other man was a disappointment?

When no one could compare to this man?

I couldn't focus on my lips on his because he felt so good between my legs. My mouth rested against his, and I breathed through the pleasure, feeling like a real woman when I was stretched like this. "Maverick..." I could feel the tears in my eyes already, feel the climax before it even arrived.

His eyes looked into mine, as if he was waiting for the tears to fall. "I love it when you cry, Sheep."

---

I sat at the dinner table alone, hoping Maverick would join me. He'd been at the office all day, on the opposite side of his property inside the factory where he made Italy's most exclusive cheese.

Abigail set the table—for one.

"Maverick won't be joining me?" She seemed to be the only person who knew anything about his schedule.

"No. He's working late." She set the basket of bread in front of me, along with a new bottle of wine.

After the sex we'd had, it seemed like everything was fine.

Our old relationship had returned, and our connection had stabilized. We weren't enemies anymore. I didn't want to sleep around with men who would only disappoint me, so that meant I wanted to be with Maverick more...but there were boundaries. We couldn't be regular lovers, just casual sex. If it ever escalated into anything more, he would push me away instantly. "Have you seen Caspian?"

"Not since the day he and Maverick bloodied each other." She poured the wine then left the bottle on the table.

"Where does Caspian live? Is he close by?"

She straightened then raised an eyebrow, confused by my question. "Why?"

"I know Maverick hasn't talked to him, and I wish they could work it out."

"Mr. DeVille is stubborn. And his father is even more stubborn. I don't think their story has a happy ending. Ever since his wife died, that man hasn't been the same. Not to me, any of the other servants, and definitely not to his kids."

I'd forgotten Maverick had a sister. He never talked about her. "Maybe I could talk to him..."

"And get yourself killed?" she asked incredulously. "That won't do anyone any good—unless you kill him on your way down." She didn't hide her venom for the man who was so cold to Maverick. She clearly had great affection for her employer.

"I just want to talk...not fight."

"I don't think you'll have the option."

I wanted to press her for information, but I knew I wouldn't get anything. She was far too loyal to Maverick to give me any help. And if she knew what I had in mind, she would tattle on me right away. "Thank you for dinner."

---

I sat on the couch in my room with the TV on. It was getting late, and I suspected Maverick was home by now. A part of me hoped he would come to my bedroom, even if it was just for a quick chat. But the silence continued, leading me to believe such a visit would never take place.

I grabbed my phone and texted him. *Do you have company for the evening?* This man was so handsome, so confident, and so sexy that he was magnetic. He attracted the attention of every person in the room, like honey attracting a swarm of bees. Finding a beautiful woman for a night of meaningless passion was easier than opening a bottle of wine. He could get laid whenever he was in the mood. So it wouldn't surprise me if he were already with someone else, forgetting about our night together like it didn't happen.

A few minutes passed before the three dots popped up on my phone. *No.*

My heart gave a slight thump in excitement. *Do you want company...?*

*I always want to fuck—if that's what you're asking.*

I didn't just want sex. I wanted to spend time with him, ask him about his day. I wanted to share a bottle of wine and run my fingers through his dark hair. I wanted connection, intimacy.

I went upstairs and stepped inside his bedroom.

He was sitting up in bed, wearing just his sweatpants as his powerful back leaned against the headboard. His ankles were crossed, and his bare feet reached toward the end of the bed, athletic with a prominent arch. Every feature he possessed was somehow masculine, somehow sexy. An iPad was sitting in his lap, and his eyes were glued to the screen like he was reading something.

I shut the door behind me and stepped inside.

He finished reading whatever held his attention then he lifted his gaze to meet mine. His hair was still styled from his shower, and his jaw was clean from his shave. He watched me with those eyes that reminded me of a hot cup of coffee on a cold morning. They were penetrative, intimate. He set aside his device without taking his eyes off me.

I moved to the other side of the bed and stripped out of my clothes, keeping my panties on.

His eyes trailed over my body, examining the curve of my tits and my waistline. He seemed to like the white color of my underwear, the way it matched my pale skin. His eyes were focused on me, slowly turning from calm to intense.

I pulled back the sheets and slipped into bed beside him. The second my body softened into the mattress, I felt comfortable. The mattress was probably identical to the one I had in my bedroom, but his felt so much better. With my body turned on the side, I looked up at the beautiful man who hadn't taken his eyes off me.

He finally scooted down then turned over, his head resting on the pillow right beside me. He didn't ravish me right away, taking his time as he undressed me with his gaze. His cologne was fragrant, the scent that made ovaries melt.

My hand moved to his chest, and my fingers pressed into the area where two slabs of muscles met right in the center. Slowly, my hand explored until it found the drumbeat of his heart, the gentle thump as his body worked to stay alive. He was warm to the touch, scorching hot. My eyes followed my movements, appreciating all of his beauty. "How was your day?"

"I thought you came here for sex."

"I did. But I still want to know how your day was."

He turned contemplative, like he considered ignoring the question. "I had a lot of shipments go out today. Some of my wheels have aged to perfection, and now everyone wants them. They had to be loaded onto the truck for delivery."

"You help with that?"

"No. I just make sure it gets done. I have foremen who help with management, but my father taught me that if you want things done right, you have to do them yourself…and he was right."

My fingers glided down to his hard stomach, feeling the hard grooves. "Have you spoken to your father?"

"No. And when I do, I know it won't be pleasant."

"Have you considered reaching out to him? You know, soften the tension."

His eyes were nearly the color of his hair, deep brown. His tanned skin reminded me of olive oil, so stunning. "Softness is weakness in my world. It's essential to be respected—especially by your enemies."

"Your father is your enemy?"

He gave a slow nod. "Unfortunately."

"I hope it won't always be that way." Especially since I was the reason they were pitted against each other. The last time they were in the same room together, it seemed like one of them was going to die.

If he was still angry with me, he didn't show it. "My father is stubborn."

"Only because he's upset. He's not thinking rationally."

"Doesn't matter."

I wished there were something I could do to repair the damage between them, to bring father and son back to the same side. Caspian was despicable, but he was still Maverick's father. I wanted them to have the relationship I had with my father…to be close. "What's your sister's name?"

A slight reaction took place on his face, a dilation of his eyes. He wasn't as relaxed as he was a moment ago, the subject making him tense. He'd never talked about her before, only mentioned her in passing. "Lily."

"Pretty name…"

"She's a pretty girl."

My lips slightly lifted into a smile, moved by what he said. "You two are close?"

His eyes dropped. "We've gotten closer since my mother died. Dealing with our father made us allies. We're both hardheaded and stubborn, so we didn't always get along. But you know what they say, tragedy always brings people together…"

"I've never seen her come by the house before. Do you see her often?"

He kept his gaze averted. "No."

"Why? Does she live somewhere else?"

He turned back to me, hostility in his gaze. "You ask a lot of questions."

"Just curious… You know everything about me."

"I doubt that."

"I'm not asking to be nosy. I just like talking to you." It was easy to look past his rough edges when I knew how good he was underneath. He was protective and honest, the kind of qualities any woman would want in a man. When he let his walls come down, he was irresistible.

"She's here in Florence—but she's in rehab." He watched my gaze and studied my reaction.

It was hard to stay stoic when the information was so surprising. "Oh…I'm sorry." I'd never dealt with addiction or knew anyone with a problem. But I saw Maverick drink like he could easily be addicted himself.

"She and my mother were really close. It wasn't just her death that devastated her. It was also how she died…it really disturbed my sister. She quickly slid into drinking. When she developed a tolerance for that, she moved on to something stronger…and just slipped away. My father made it worse and pushed her to her breaking point. To this day, he's never visited her in rehab. He's never even talked to her about it…just disowned her. Apparently, it's too hard to pick up the phone and check on your own fucking daughter."

Bitterness exploded out of his mouth like a burst of flame. "So, now it's just the two of us...and I have to be what she needs."

He seemed to take care of everyone around him, including me. But who took care of him? "She's lucky to have you."

"I'm all she's got." He looked away again, his eyes filled with sad thoughts. "This is why I prefer fucking instead of talking. Nothing good ever comes from talking." His eyes shifted back to mine, a little darker than before.

My hand slid to his arm, my fingertips gently sliding over the mounds of muscle. "That's too bad...because I like talking to you." I slid my body closer to his and hooked my leg over his hip, bringing our faces just inches apart. My hand slid into the hair at the back of his neck, and my fingers caressed the soft strands. The instant I started to touch him this way, he relaxed a bit. It seemed to be his favorite spot, his weakness.

His eyes stayed on mine, a little less hostile than before. His hand rested on my thigh and slowly slid up to my ass, his large fingers warm to the touch. When he reached my thong, he gently tugged on the lace, like he wanted to pull it off.

When I came to his bedroom, sex wasn't the biggest issue on my mind. When he had been seriously injured, we lay in bed and watched movies all day, forced to cuddle and talk. That's what I wanted the most from him, to have that kind of relationship. After I'd pissed him off, it disappeared. Slowly, it began to rebuild, his anger fading away.

I wanted to look in those beautiful eyes forever, but the comfort started to soften me, started to make me slip away.

My eyes closed and my fingers halted in his hair, locked around the strands I loved to play with. This house was an impenetrable fortress, but I never felt as safe as I did when I was by his side.

It only took me a minute to drift off to that moment between consciousness and sleep. I was on the edge, about to tip over and fall into the abyss. That was when I felt Maverick's movements. He pulled the sheets down and over my body, spreading them on top of me and tucking me in. Then I heard the click of the bedside lamp as he turned off the light. His body returned to mine, and he lay in the same position as before, tugging my leg over his hip.

Then he let me sleep.

## 4

## MAVERICK

I pulled through the open gates and approached the two-story castle. Just like my estate, my father's place was situated in the countryside, still living in the same home he'd shared with my mother.

Sometimes I worried it was poisoning his mind. Her ghost haunted the hallways. Her presence in the walls and furniture constantly reminded him of what he'd lost. He turned his injured mind into a madhouse.

Just as I stepped out of the car, he strode out the house. Summer was over, and fall was subtly rolling in. A night like this would still have been filled with heat just a month ago, but now it had touches of coolness. He wore a black jacket over his collared shirt, his dark hair matching his mood.

I walked toward him, my gun stuffed into the back of my jeans. It was loaded and ready to fire. All I had to do was click off the safety. I'd never thought I needed protection around my father, but now I saw him as a serious threat.

He'd nearly killed me at the house—and he would have killed my wife if I hadn't stopped him.

He stopped in front of me, several feet in between us since this was a hostile meeting. The outdoor lights provided enough illumination so I could see the sour look on his face—and I was sure he could see mine. He was probably packing under that jacket. Why else would he be wearing it?

He was the one who had called this meeting, so I stood silently as I waited for him to speak first. Maybe this was all a ploy to kill me, to take a cheap shot under the flag of truce. If he were anyone else, I would eliminate him immediately. It was always a bad idea to let a threat go unchecked. But our shared blood made me soft, made me hope for a more optimistic resolution.

He stared at me with the same hatred, like he was ashamed I carried the DeVille surname. With beady black eyes that blended in with the night, he watched me without blinking. "Have you put her down yet?"

His men kept tabs on Arwen and me, so he already knew the answer to his question. He was just trying to make a point. "Arwen is different from us. She saw two innocent women who needed to be rescued—so she rescued them. I know that thwarted your plans, but it wasn't personal."

His eyes narrowed. "You aren't a teenager anymore, Maverick. Why are you still so weak for pussy?"

I stood my ground and didn't react, even though it was such a crass thing for a father to say to a son. "You're the one who made me marry her. All of this happened because of you. You brought a stranger into the family. If you hadn't done that, then she wouldn't have let the girls go. Cause and effect."

He took a step closer to me. "It was necessary."

"We would have found Ramon on our own—eventually."

"If she's such a burden, then put a bullet in her damn head. Be done with it." His hands hung at his sides, and they both tightened into fists. "All she had to do was keep her head down and shut her mouth, and she would have had a nice life. She's lucky to wear such a respected surname as DeVille. But if she doesn't understand loyalty, she doesn't deserve it. Put her in the ground."

Her father was long gone, and she did betray my family when she snuck around behind my back. She hijacked our plans and took matters into her own hands. If one of our men did the same, they would be executed. We had every right to dispose of her, to give her the ultimate punishment. I'd be a bachelor once more, having that house to myself without a wife to protect. She was a woman who easily attracted the obsession of men, so I had to chase them away with my frightening growls and sharp teeth. Not to mention, I had a seven-foot mutant to worry about now. Killing her was the pragmatic choice. It was a choice I was justified to make.

"Maverick." My father lowered his voice, turning lethal. "Kill her."

I could go home right now and put a bullet in her head. I could stand over her bed while she was sound asleep. She wouldn't even know what happened because it would be over so quickly.

He took another step closer to me. "Did you hear me?"

It was dead silent in the middle of the night. Of course I heard him.

"She doesn't deserve your protection, Maverick. She's a two-timing whore. She deserves to die a whore's death."

My eyes narrowed on his face, unnerved by the insult she didn't deserve.

"Kill her. Or I'll kill you." Now, we were close together, our eyes locked and full of menace. "Put that bitch in the ground, or I'll do it myself. And then I'll throw you in with her."

My father had threatened to kill me several times now, and each one was more painful than the last. Without my mother on this earth, I was easily expendable. There was no love in his gaze, no affection in his heart. At least Arwen remembered my birthday. At least Arwen asked how my day was. At least she was there for me when this demon never was. "I choose her."

The rage that took over his face was indescribable. Two explosions happened in his eyes, and his eyebrows furrowed as if he couldn't believe what I'd just said. Like a billowing cloud about to drop a storm, his eyes grew darker and darker.

"Goodbye, Caspian." I turned my back to him, knowing there was a serious chance he would draw on me and put a bullet in my back. But if my father really did such a thing, I wouldn't have much motivation to live anyway. I'd lost my mother, my sister was in rehab, and my father disowned me. I had no one.

There was only one family member left, one person who shared my name.

My wife.

---

I WORKED around the clock for the next few days. As long as I stayed busy, I didn't think about the threat Caspian had unleashed. He wanted to murder my wife and toss my body in with hers. I wasn't afraid of death because I saw it as merciful. When the human body collapsed under intense pain, opting out was the best gift that could be given.

But it disturbed me that my own father wanted to murder me.

If my mother were still alive, she'd beat the shit out of him.

I finished dinner with a client in the city, one of my big vendors that operated restaurants throughout the country. We talked numbers and increasing production to meet those demands, and then we parted ways.

I walked to my car in the darkness, thinking about the business I'd just grabbed. When my family business had existed in the underworld, our lives had revolved around money, drugs, and territory. The cheese business took a back seat. But now it was my only priority since I had become a law-abiding citizen. It was a much more relaxing livelihood.

But I couldn't enjoy it because I had two psychopaths for enemies.

I turned the corner and was approaching my Bugatti when my phone rang in my pocket. I glanced at the screen and saw Arwen's name. I got into the car, started the engine, and then took the call through the car. "Yes?"

"We haven't spoken in three days, and that's how you greet me?"

I turned the car around and sped through the streets, driving like an asshole because I was an asshole. The corner of my mouth rose in a smile at her attitude, noting the way she told me off when others were too scared to do the same. "It's been a long day."

"I doubt it."

With one hand on the wheel, I tried to focus on the road instead of picturing her beautiful face. She was probably at home in her bedroom, wondering when I would be back. "Is there something you needed?"

"Do I have to need something to talk to you?"

I wasn't used to this kind of relationship, where I had someone I spoke to on a daily basis. We didn't discuss business or crime. We didn't discuss anything in particular, just as I would with a friend. She became someone in my inner circle, someone like Kent. But I also fucked her...which was interesting. "Most people want something from me."

"Well, I want to talk to you. I guess that's something."

My eyes stayed on the road, but my mind was focused on the sound of her voice. Even when she wasn't singing, the tone of her words was heavenly. If I didn't know she was a singer, I would have guessed it just by listening to her talk. It was soothing to my ears, calming my irritated nerves and dropping my blood pressure. Having an affectionate wife should irritate me, but I appreciated her concern...considering my own father didn't give a damn about me. "And what do you want to talk about?"

"How about we start with your day?"

My mother used to ask me that when I came home from school. She even asked me that when she called me as an adult. Even though it was undeniable that I had aged into a grizzled man, she still talked to me as if I'd just walked in the door from school. It used to annoy me, but now I missed it. "I just finished dinner with a client. He wants to place a big order, but since the production process is so finite, it's complicated. We found a solution to the problem."

"That sounds fun. Talking about cheese over dinner isn't a bad way to make a living."

And being the wife of a rich man wasn't a bad way to make a living either.

"What are you doing now?"

"Driving home."

"Alone?" There was a slight hesitation in her voice, as if she feared there was a woman sitting in the passenger seat at that very moment.

"Yes. Too tired to hit the bars."

"It doesn't seem like you've been home much for the last few days. What have you been up to?"

"Why does this feel like an interrogation?"

"It's not. Like it or not, you're my closest friend, Maverick."

I'd noticed the way she'd become closer to me, coming into my room to talk rather than screw. She texted me more often than she used to, telling me about her day when I didn't ask. "I've been working a lot."

"A lot is an understatement."

"Alright...I've been working nonstop."

"It seems like you're avoiding me..."

She hit the nail right on the head. "Because I am."

"Why is that?"

I didn't want to have this conversation on the phone while I was speeding through the countryside in my expensive car. "I'll be home in fifteen minutes. We'll talk then."

---

I GREETED Abigail then headed up the stairs.

Arwen was on the second landing waiting for me. She was in silk pajama shorts that barely covered her ass and a white tank top that was so thin, it showed the outline of her nipples. Her skimpy clothes showcased the curves of her frame, the feminine beauty of her gorgeous body.

I almost forgot why she was waiting for me.

I walked past her and kept going, pretending to be unimpressed.

She came up behind me and followed me into my bedroom.

When I got inside, I immediately started to take off my slacks and collared shirt. She'd seen me naked so many times that I felt comfortable stripping like she wasn't there at all. When the buttons were undone, I peeled off the shirt and tossed it onto the armchair.

Her shiny hair was pulled into a high ponytail, and her makeup had already been washed off for the night. Her fair skin had a natural glow to it, like the moon as it reflected the light from the sun. Her blue eyes watched my movements, dissecting everything I did like she knew me better than anyone. "So?"

"So." I dropped my pants and stripped down to my boxers.

She moved into me, coming so close she might kiss me. Her perfume was still fragrant, and she smelled like flowers, roses on a summer day. She was nearly a foot shorter than me in heels, so she moved her face into my chest.

I watched her, unsure what she was doing.

Her arms encircled my waist, and she rested her cheek against my chest, hugging me.

I stood there as she blanketed me with affection, ignoring the fact that I'd just told her I'd been avoiding her. The insult didn't seem to offend her, not if she still wanted to hold me. With my arms by my sides, I continued to stand there and wait for her to finish.

When I didn't return her affection, she pulled away. "You won't even hug your wife when you get home?"

"I didn't realize we had the type of relationship that included hugging."

She crossed her arms over her chest, her eyebrow raised. "You can't accept a compliment just the way you can't accept affection. Your father really did a number on you…"

I'd never considered my behavior to be a reflection of my relationship with my father—but I knew she was right. During my final conversation with him, he threatened to kill me...and it wasn't the first time that had ever happened.

"Why are you avoiding me?" Once I'd rejected her, she turned cold, getting right to the point.

Sometimes I resented her because of my growing attraction. Instead of getting sick of her like most women, I desired her more. And when she wore that tiny little outfit, it made me hard in my boxers, and since the material wasn't thick, she could see it if she looked down. The more I allowed her into my life, the more I hated it. "I saw my father a couple of nights ago."

"Oh...that must have been fun."

"Yeah...that's one way to describe it."

She shifted her weight to one hip, waiting for me to explain further.

"He told me to kill you." He'd made his desires transparent. If I wanted to keep my relationship with my dad, I had to show him my loyalty. That meant I had to execute her...as if she were one of our men who crossed us. He didn't seem to understand right from wrong, or the difference between man and woman. He wanted her to face the same consequences as someone else...but that wouldn't be right.

Her eyes shifted back and forth as she looked at me, clearly unnerved by my confession.

"I said no."

She tried to keep her face stoic, but her shoulders relaxed as she released the air from her lungs.

"Now, we're enemies. This will only end one way—when one of us is dead."

She shook her head slightly, her eyes filled with pain. "He's so far gone…"

He wasn't a man I recognized at all.

She stepped toward me again. "Why did you say no?"

Killing her would have been easier. She knew that. I didn't have a good explanation. Why would any man choose a woman over his father? I wasn't a man with a moral compass. I would have let those women be raped and tortured in the barn without losing sleep. But I chose to protect this woman. "I made a promise to your father."

She raised an eyebrow. "But that promise changed when I crossed you…I know that now."

"Do you want me to kill you?" I asked incredulously.

"No. But we both know that isn't the reason." She stepped closer to me, moving in on me just the way my father did a few nights ago. "So, what is the reason? The real reason?" Her arms dropped to her sides, and she looked up at me with those beautiful eyes.

I held her gaze and didn't blink. "Those women didn't deserve to suffer. You made the right call—even though you betrayed me to do it."

"That didn't answer my question, Maverick." She hardly blinked as she stared at me, pressing for an answer she wanted to hear. "You've declared war with your father because of me. Why is my life that important?"

She'd phrased the question powerfully, giving me no wiggle room. I held her gaze with a hard dick between my legs, susceptible to the attitude in her voice, the fire in her eyes. "If I didn't declare war with him now, it would just happen later. Like you said, he's too far gone. It doesn't matter whether I make a stand now or later...but I choose now."

"And it has nothing to do with the way you feel about me?" She circled closer, not giving up. Now her face was close to mine, close enough that I could see every detail of her beautiful features. "Because I've come to care for you, Maverick. I think you care about me too."

I became her husband because I'd been forced. It was a role I'd never wanted, but I fell into it easily because she needed me so much. She needed me to guide her during our first dance as husband and wife. She needed me to take care of her father when she couldn't afford his medical bills. She needed me to hold her hand when he died. She needed me for everything—and I was there for her. It started as an obligation but quickly became a way of life. Now I was used to taking care of her, used to checking on her. And I was used to having someone care about me too. "I don't want you to die..."

Her hands moved to my arms, her fingertips lightly pressing into my skin. She closed the gap between us and rose onto her tiptoes so we could be eye to eye. Then she closed her eyes and rested her face against mine.

We stood there together, neither one of us saying a word.

My eyes closed and I relished the feeling of her cheek on

mine, feeling whatever pull existed between us. This woman was barely my friend and barely my lover, but she somehow meant something to me. I was a heartless man who preferred the easy way out, but this time, I chose the hard way. I chose to protect my sheep.

Her lips moved to mine, landing on my mouth perfectly. The kiss was subtle, gentle. Her lips felt mine, waiting for me to reciprocate before she kissed me any harder. When my lips didn't move, she pulled back and looked me in the eye.

"I do care about you, Sheep..."

## 5

## ARWEN

Maverick's weight pressed me into the mattress. He covered me completely, holding up his body on his powerful arms as his hips thrust to move inside me. Covered in sweat from the exertion and with a sexy look in his eyes, he was the ideal man to be on top of a woman. He rocked his body over and over, his length burrowing inside me until his balls tapped lightly against my ass. The sex was slow, our bodies moving together at an unremarkable speed.

But the sex was so good. My toes were cramping over and over, and my nipples were sore because they'd been hard for so long. My knees were wide apart, giving him plenty of access to move between my thighs and enjoy me.

For the second time, I came. I whimpered against his mouth, my eyes stinging with tears once more. They burned as they built up then streaked down my cheeks to my lips. I'd never been a crier in bed, but this man brought me to tears every single time. It was always so good that it was heavenly, like I should be thanking someone upstairs.

The condom separated us, but I could still feel the hard grooves of his dick, especially the large crown at the top. Sometimes I wished we were just skin-to-skin, but I knew the request wasn't optional. So, I enjoyed it as-is...because it was still so good.

Maverick wore the sexiest look in bed, focused on the woman he was with, while keeping his fit body in motion. He seemed more aroused by the expressions I made than the way my tits shook back and forth. Sometimes he would moan, but for the most part, he was a quiet lover, choosing to listen to me instead of being vocal himself.

But when he came, it was always so sexy.

His jaw clenched, almost as if he were angry about something. Then his eyes smoldered, treasuring the pleasure in his body before he exploded between my legs. His chest puffed up as he took in a deep breath to hold. Then he shuddered as his body took over, as his hips bucked to get his dick deeper inside me while he finished. His forehead rested against mine, and he moaned as he came, a little louder than usual.

My fingers snaked into his hair, and I caressed the strands as I felt him relax. My husband was the best lover I'd ever had, and watching him find the same satisfaction turned me on. I wanted him to feel as good as I did, to love fucking me as much as I loved fucking him.

After a few more seconds of rest, he rolled off me and cleaned off in the bathroom.

I lay in his big, comfortable bed, ready to fall asleep.

He came back minutes later, naked and beautiful. He got

into bed beside me but didn't cuddle with me. He'd only done that once and hadn't done it again since. Now that the sex was over, he was distant. He seemed to be doing it on purpose, as if forcing himself to draw an invisible boundary in our relationship. Sometimes he let me get closer to him, but if I got too close, he pulled away.

I opened my eyes and looked at him, spotting the coldness in his eyes. Our tender moment was long gone. To him, it had already been forgotten. "Maverick?" I propped myself up, my head resting against my palm.

He stared at the ceiling, one hand behind his head while the other rested on his chest. "Yes?"

"Has there ever been a serious woman in your life?"

The air around him turned noticeably tenser, like he had sucked all the life and joy from the room. "I don't ask you about your past, so why ask about mine?"

"That's what friends do." He immediately turned into the spitting image of his father, but I didn't have the heart to tell him something so insulting—even if it was true. "I've had a few men in my life, but nothing too serious. I've loved boys in the past, but when I look back on them, I realize that wasn't love. It was just… I don't know."

"I didn't ask."

"Maverick, come on."

He turned his head toward me, his eyes cold.

"It's three steps forward and two steps back. Every time."

He knew exactly what I meant, so he faced the ceiling again.

"Stop pretending you don't care about me. Stop pretending our relationship doesn't make you happy."

He clenched his jaw but didn't make a rebuttal. "No, I've never been in love."

"Ever had a girlfriend?"

He was quiet for a long time. "No."

"So, when you lost your virginity, that was a one-night stand too?" I asked incredulously, assuming he had to have had some meaningful relationship in his life.

"That was just a fuck in the back seat of a car. You're the closest thing I've ever had to a relationship."

"So, only when you were forced to get married did you actually try to get to know someone?"

He shrugged. "I'm not much of a talker. I'm an even worse listener."

"I don't think that's true..."

He kept his eyes on the ceiling.

"Why are you like that?"

"Why is anyone the way they are?" he asked. "No one really knows."

"Well, why don't you want a relationship with a woman?"

"I don't like anyone," he blurted. "That's just how I am. I'm not a big people person. Being in a relationship requires talking and dates... I can barely get out a few sentences all day. And I can barely listen to a woman speak for five minutes without losing my libido. So, I strike fast. Get what I need, then get out."

"So, it has nothing to do with sowing your oats?"

He shrugged. "I guess not. What did you see in Dante?"

"He was handsome, kind…and he was good to me." I hadn't thought about him in a while. He was probably happy with the woman he'd replaced me with. He'd probably pitied me in the beginning, but now I was just a distant memory.

"He wasn't that good…if you ask me."

"It just wasn't meant to be. I don't blame him for walking away."

"I do. Coward."

I dropped my hand and returned my body to the bed, my hair stretching across the pillow. "Before all of this happened, he used to talk about us getting married and having two kids. But everything changed the second I put on this ring."

He didn't say anything to that.

Since he was in a dark mood, I stopped talking. His attitude could change within a few heartbeats. Now he was brooding in his silence, thinking about something he would never share with me.

"I'm sorry about your father… I know it must be hard."

Slowly, he turned his head back to me.

"Even if he is wrong, even if he is an ass, he's still your father…and I'm sorry." I wasn't entirely to blame for the divide. His father had turned into an asshole a long time ago. I was the only one who'd stood up to him, who'd done the right thing when even Maverick didn't care, but I didn't want to see my husband suffer.

"Whatever."

I knew it hurt him more than that, but he obviously didn't want to talk about it. "Maybe you should tell your sister what's going on."

"Like she doesn't have enough on her plate already."

"It's still good to tell her...in case he contacts her. I was also hoping I could meet her."

He kept watching me, slightly surprised by what I'd just offered. "Why would you want to do that?"

"She's my sister-in-law, right?"

"Because of a sham marriage."

Like a drop of acid in my eyes, the comment burned. "Still... until death do us part. If she's important to you, she's important to me."

He faced forward again, his eyes on the ceiling. He turned contemplative, his mind a million miles away. Even though there was only a foot between us on the bed, it seemed like we were on different planets. "I'll think about it."

---

TODAY HAD BEEN a lot harder than I expected.

I'd been dreading it all week, but I didn't think it would be as painful as I feared.

Somehow, it was.

I drove to a flower shop in the city and stared blankly at the selections, unsure what to get. Knowing my father, it wouldn't matter. He would tell me not to waste money on something he would never see.

But it made all the difference in the world to me.

On the verge of tears and unable to make a decision between the selections, I just grabbed a bouquet at random and paid for it. By the time I made it to my car, my tears had destroyed my flawless makeup.

Was I an idiot to think I could do this alone?

I hadn't been to my father's grave since the funeral, and of course, Maverick had been with me. With his hand holding mine and strength in his touch, he'd carried me through that day because I was too weak to do it myself.

Now I realized I couldn't do this without him.

I needed him like I needed air.

I stemmed my tears and made the call, the phone pressed to my ear as I watched people walk up and down the sidewalk. It was a sunny day and the temperature was mild. The phone rang as I waited for him to answer.

When it seemed like voice mail was about to pick up, he answered. "What is it?" Fiery and pissed off, he sounded like his day wasn't going well. Men spoke in the background, running their mouths as they argued about something.

"Uh...everything okay?"

"Arwen, I've got shit to do, and I don't have time for a heartfelt conversation. Call me when you actually need something."

Shocked by the cold way he spoke to me, I was nearly speechless. Tears were in my eyes once again, and the shock constricted my throat. It was difficult to get any words out, so I was only able to say one. "Okay..."

He hung up.

I set the phone in the center console and felt the tears burn my eyes. Drops of sorrow ran down my cheeks, and I felt stupid for calling him. Maybe I could never trust Maverick to be the same person every single day. He changed too much, flipped a switch without notice. I wiped my tears away and got on the road, my chest tight because of the pain.

My phone started to ring. His name was on the screen.

I was in full sobbing mode, so I ignored it, wanting nothing to do with him. I was an idiot for thinking I could call and ask him for support. I'd become used to his kindness, but I'd forgotten how quickly it evaporated.

He called again.

I ignored it.

I was just a few miles from the cemetery when he called for the third time. He'd ended our conversation so abruptly that I didn't understand why he wanted to talk to me so much now. Did he realize he was an ass the second he hung up on me?

I got tired of listening to the phone ring through the car system, so I answered. "What?" I kept my voice strong and disguised my tears as best as possible, but I was still heartbroken that the one person I relied on was so cold to me. I shouldn't have allowed myself to count on him in the first place.

There was a long pause. "What's wrong?"

"Nothing..." This time, I could hear silence in the background, as if he'd excused himself from whatever business he was doing to give me more than a few seconds of his time. Hot tears rolled down my face and slowly approached my lips, full of my heartbreak. Now I wasn't sure what I was more miserable about—the date or my husband.

"Your GPS shows you leaving Florence but going in the opposite direction of the house. Where are you going?"

I didn't care to answer him. "I know you're busy, Maverick. I'll just talk to you later." Now I couldn't disguise my tears, and they escaped in my voice, carrying my devastation on my vocal cords.

"Sheep." He stopped me from hanging up on him with just his voice. "I'm sorry I was an ass, alright? I've just got a lot on my plate right now."

"That's fine. I'll let you go—"

"Don't you fucking hang up on me."

I drove farther into the countryside, the flowers in the passenger seat.

"Talk to me, Sheep. What's going on?"

"It's my father's birthday... I was going to the cemetery to visit. I thought maybe...never mind. I know you have more important things to do, so I'll talk to you later." Before he could yell at me through the speakers, I hung up.

I kept driving and didn't hear the phone ring.

The fight was over.

When I approached the gates, he called me again.

If he called me just to scream at me for hanging up on him, I'd crash this nice car into a tree just to piss him off. "What?"

He took a long pause. "I'll be there in fifteen minutes, alright?"

That wasn't what I expected him to say. "You don't have to—"

"I want to."

"Maverick, it sounds like you're busy. I'm sure you have things to do."

"You're more important. You're always more important…and I'm sorry I didn't make that clear."

---

WHEN HE ARRIVED fifteen minutes later, I got out of my car with my flowers in hand. I'd cleaned up my makeup as best as I could in the car, but the puffiness of my eyes couldn't be hidden. The mascara had dissolved into my skin and gave it a blue tint that made me look particularly pale. That morning, I'd thought my makeup and hair had turned out perfect…but now I looked like a train wreck.

Maverick looked exactly the same as usual, masculine, fit, and strong. With his brown eyes glued to my face, he walked toward me, dressed in a black t-shirt with matching jeans. His shiny watch was on his wrist, and his jeans fit his muscular legs perfectly. Apology was in his gaze, like he knew he'd fucked up.

I was embarrassed that I'd called him in the first place, that I'd allowed a man to understand how much I needed him. If it were anyone else, I would keep my pride and never shed a tear. When Dante dumped me, I didn't have a reaction. Even when Dante was mine, I never asked him for anything. He came to the hospital to comfort me, but he did that entirely on his own. I was a proud woman who refused to admit any kind of weakness. But since the beginning, it'd been different with Maverick. I relied on him like a wife relied on her husband.

He came to my side, and his arm immediately wrapped around my waist. He took the flowers from my hand and pulled me in for a gentle kiss on the lips. It was the first time he'd greeted me like I actually meant something to him, the first time he'd held me like his wife under the sun.

He pulled away then guided me to my father's resting place.

He placed the flowers on the grave, directly under my father's name. Then he came to my side and wrapped his arm around my waist once more, becoming my rock the way he was last time. He squeezed me into his side and stayed quiet, not re-opening the conversation we'd had in the car.

I stared at my father's name and felt new tears emerge. "He was only fifty-seven…" He'd died so young, far too soon. Maybe if he'd seen a doctor sooner, things would have been different. Maybe he wanted it to be this way because he knew he didn't have any other options. My hand covered my mouth to stifle my tears when they became too much. I'd already grieved at his funeral and in the weeks afterward. Now, it started all over again, like a scab that had been picked at until it bled. "He would be fifty-eight today."

Maverick's hand squeezed my waist, holding me close to him as the tears streamed down my cheeks. He kept his silence, letting me cry and express my pain.

My mother's name was next to my father's, and sometimes I couldn't believe that she'd been gone for so long. Five years came and went. I hoped they were together in heaven, their spirits playing in the clouds.

I stood there for thirty minutes, and not once did Maverick say a word or drop his comfort. He was there for me just the way he was before. If he had somewhere to be, he didn't admit it. It seemed like he had all day to stand there beside me.

When my tears finally ran dry and my heart was stitched back together, I turned away. "I'm ready to go..." I turned my back on the grave and walked to the black car, wondering how my father would feel about Maverick if he were still alive. When Caspian wanted to kill me, Maverick stayed on my side. It was something I had to remember on his bad days, that he was a good man underneath that hostility.

He walked me to my car door. "You want to get something to eat? Something to get your mind thinking about something else?"

I didn't have an appetite at all. The only thing I wanted to do was go home and press my fingers to the keys of the piano. Music got me through my darkest times. "No. I think I'm just going to go home." I opened the door.

He closed it. "I'm here. Use me." He placed his body in front of the door so I couldn't open it again. He forced me to back up, to move to the rear of the car. We were the only visitors to the cemetery, so we could have any conversation we wanted. Not even the dead could hear us. "I'm sorry I was an ass to you before. If I'd known you needed me, I wouldn't have talked to you that way."

"How about you just stop talking that way anyway? Sounds like a good rule of thumb." The criticism flew out of my mouth quickly, my suppressed rage taking the reins.

He obviously pitied me when he didn't fire back. "I'll work on it…"

I was frustrated about my life, disappointed this was where I'd ended up. Both of my parents were gone, and I was married to a man who would never be more than my friend and occasional lover. My life felt stale.

He studied me, one hand resting on top of the car. "If it makes any difference, I really do feel like shit. I hate watching you cry…"

"You told me you liked it."

"In a very different context." He lowered his hand, his eyes still focused on me. "I wouldn't have picked you over my father if I didn't care about you. Hearing your tears through the phone was like glass scraping against a chalkboard."

"If that's the case, stop flipping back and forth. Stop being kind to me one minute and then cold the next."

"Sorry…it's just how I am."

"Well, that's not how you should be with me. You can trust me and I can trust you. We're all each other has now…"

That seemed to mean something to him because his eyes softened. He went from being a brooding man to being a kind soul. "I've never been married before…I'm not sure how this works."

"If you aren't going to kill me, then this is a lifetime commitment. That means we need to be good to each other, every single day. We need to be there for each other. We need to trust each other. Stop keeping me at a distance, and let me in. I'm the most reliable person in your life right now."

He fit in with the Tuscan countryside behind him, a beautiful Italian man with great appreciation for the soil, the trees, and the gorgeous landscape that surrounded us every day. He drank wine like water, he perfected cheese for a living, and he knew how to make love like a man passionately in love. "I'm not good at letting people in. I don't think I'll ever be good at it."

"Why not?"

He turned his gaze and surveyed the fields around us, Florence in the distance. "I've lost my mother…my sister… and now my father. I've had my heart broken too many times."

"But you haven't lost your sister and your father."

"My sister is a completely different person now. Our relationship isn't the same. Memories that I have with my family will need to be locked in a vault because I'll never make new ones. My mother was the nucleus that held us all together, and the second she was gone, we all broke apart. I don't need to explain that my father is different too…that I'm not a son to him. Even the tightest relationships fall apart. Friends say they'll be close forever, and then life gets in the way… and they don't speak for years. Nothing ever stays the same, nothing is ever concrete. The people you love are the ones you lose." It was the longest monologue he'd ever given me, an open window into the clouded thoughts in his mind. He displayed his vulnerability and finally spoke his mind freely, showing me his old wounds and how painful they still were.

I understood his pain because I'd lost both of my parents, but he had a different kind of pain that I'd never had to carry. When my mother was gone, my father was still there. But every member of his family quickly disappeared, like they'd never been there at all. He couldn't take a compliment because he hardly ever received them, and he couldn't accept love because he hadn't gotten that either. His mother's death had traumatized him in so many ways. Now he was afraid to let me in, let anyone in, because it seemed pointless. "I'm not going anywhere, Maverick."

He didn't blink as he looked at me. "Doesn't matter. My father and sister haven't gone anywhere…but they aren't the same."

## 6

## MAVERICK

It was an unusually cool evening, so I started a fire.

The flames leaped to life in the hearth and filled my bedroom with enough warmth to push the cold air through the cracks in the windows. With a glass of scotch in my hand, I took a drink as I sat up in bed, watching the flames dance.

The second I yelled at Arwen on the phone, I'd felt like shit.

Especially when I heard the tears.

I wasn't sympathetic or compassionate, but something about her pain tore me up inside. I couldn't stand it. When she sang or spoke, it was the most beautiful sound. But her tears were another story.

Work had been a nightmare because we'd increased production and made errors in the process. As a result, we lost an entire batch of product and wasted the entire day. My temperature was running hot, and she called at the wrong time.

I guess I should have controlled my anger better.

I'd never been good at that sort of thing.

A knock sounded on my bedroom door. My hand returned the glass to the nightstand, and I stared at the door, knowing Abigail wasn't the one on the other side. Arwen hadn't texted me, but she was more comfortable stopping by my bedroom when she assumed I didn't have company. "Come in."

She opened the door and came inside, in her sleep shorts with messy hair. She continued to grip the handle as she lingered in the doorway. Even though her eyes were on the bed, she didn't immediately dive for it.

I was in my boxers as I sat on the mattress, getting ready for bed even though I wasn't tired. Now that she'd walked in the door, wearing shorts that let her ass hang out, I was even less tired. But after the day we'd had, I suspected she wasn't in the mood for sex. And after being such an ass, I would be wrong to demand it.

She continued to stand at the door, like she was afraid to ask for what she wanted.

I grabbed the sheets beside me and pushed them down, inviting her to sleep.

She shut the door then crawled into my bed. Her sexy legs disappeared under the cotton sheets, and she pulled the hair tie out of her ponytail so the strands would come free across the pillow. Her eyes were still puffy from all the crying she'd done that afternoon. No amount of makeup could cover it.

I slid down under the sheets then turned off the lamp at my

bedside. When the room was blanketed in darkness, the flames illuminated the walls. The gentle crackle and pop of the fire filled the silence.

She looked at the flames before she looked at me again. "Can I sleep with you tonight?"

My wife needed me, and I'd be a dick if I kicked her out. "Yeah."

She stuck to her side of the bed and didn't try to cuddle with me.

I didn't care to show affection to a woman. There was only kissing and touching before sex. Then there was just fucking. After the fun part was over, there was no reason to share another embrace. She stuck to her side of the bed, and I stuck to mine.

But I knew that wasn't what she wanted.

What she needed.

I scooted closer to her and wrapped my arm around her waist, bringing us close together under the sheets. The curve of her back was so prominent that it was easy to slide my arm into place, easy to drag her closer into me.

Her eyes opened and she visibly melted, like affection was all she needed. She rested her head against mine with her hand on my chest. Her eyes closed again, and she breathed a happy sigh, like she this was all the medicine she needed to heal.

My fingers moved into her hair, and I gently pulled the strands away from her face, showing her almond-shaped eyes and those full lips. I'd never been with a woman more than a couple of times, and I'd never slept with a woman without actually fucking her. But Arwen was a very rare exception.

She was the only woman who could get my attention and keep it.

She was the only woman who could call and ask for anything.

She was the only woman I would choose over my father.

Because she was my wife.

She carried my name and my ring, identifying herself as my property everywhere she went. It increased my social standing and gave me a sense of pride. I was heartless and idiotic at times, but I knew I had a trophy on my hands.

A priceless heirloom.

"Thank you for coming today," she whispered into the darkness, her voice barely louder than the sound of the flames.

"I'll always be there for you, Sheep." Now that I'd turned my back on my father, I really had to keep her safe. She had two enemies lurking in the darkness, two monsters that blended in with the shadows. I had to stay on guard and keep watching, protect my little sheep from being eaten.

Protect my little wife.

"You're all I have in this world...and I'm so glad my father made me marry you."

She'd despised me when we met. I could see it in her eyes, not just hear it in her words. She was the most combative woman I'd ever known, sparking an attitude from gasoline and flames. She had the fierceness that would make her a good crime lord of the underworld. Now she was singing a much different tune...turning a new key. She'd softened like a rose petal as it fell off the bud. She was delicate without her roots, vulnerable to the world around her. But she let me take care of her...needed me to take care of her. It made my dick hard to listen to her openly need me, to admit I was the only man she could rely on. It didn't just inflate my ego. It made me feel valuable.

"I didn't know what I wanted in a husband...until I met you."

---

"I DIDN'T REALIZE how much you liked to socialize." She rose out of the car and took my hand for balance. She was in a skintight dark blue dress with a mermaid cut. A diamond necklace hung around her throat, complementing the wedding ring on her left hand.

"Can't stand it." I tossed the keys to the valet then circled my arm around her waist. "But that's how the real world works. Money likes to talk to money." I guided her up the steps and down the long path that led to the front of the house. It was already lit up inside, people chatting in the windows.

"Wow, this place is beautiful."

"Once belonged to a count."

"I bet there will be people here who knew my father... Is that a problem?"

"Why would it be?"

"Because he pissed away our family inheritance."

I stopped before reached the next landing of stairs. "Couldn't care less. You don't weigh me down. People appreciate you because of your talent, not judge you because of your father's stupidity. And don't forget you're a very wealthy woman now—as a DeVille." I guided her up the stairs once more, helping her maneuver in her insane heels. Her hair was in curls and pinned to one side, and she'd done something special to her makeup to make her look particularly gorgeous. She would steal all the attention tonight.

She smiled slightly. "Well, that's a good way to put it..."

We approached the entrance with my arm around her waist, a beautiful couple that looked happy to be together. I hated these social events, but she made them easier. She stole all the focus, so people didn't want to talk to me nearly as much.

When we reached the entryway, she stared at the people mingling inside, all wearing beautiful gowns and fine suits. Everyone there was dressed in their finest, working to impress everyone else at the party.

But my wife was definitely the most impressive.

With her beautiful dark hair pinned to the side, her unblemished skin glowed like the bistro lights strung around the property. Her dress had a deep V in the front, showing off the cleavage of her perfect tits. The diamond glittered with rainbows, but it didn't distract from the beautiful woman who wore it.

It was one of my favorite dresses I'd ever seen her wear because it highlighted every sexy curve she possessed, from her waist to her ample tits. Sometimes I wondered if she was aware of how beautiful she was, if she understood that she was the most gorgeous woman in every room she entered.

It didn't seem like it.

We walked inside and were surrounded by conversations and music. A grand piano was in the corner, and a musician played light music that fit the ambiance of the party. There had to be at least five hundred people there, holding glasses of wine and champagne while appetizers were passed around.

It was bigger than the last party we went to, so her eyes were wide. "Whoa...this is a lot of people."

"And I only know about half of them."

"You know half of them?" she asked incredulously. "How can you remember that many names?"

I shrugged. "When it comes to business, the brain is always a little sharper." A waiter arrived with a tray, so I grabbed two glasses of champagne for us. "See that guy with the dark-rimmed glasses?"

She followed my gaze.

"That's Dario Nardello, the mayor of Florence." I nodded to the woman beside him. "That's his wife, Maria." With my hand on her waist, I guided Arwen farther into the room. "The blonde in the black dress is Nadia Contretti, a model known for her iconic images in Florence." I could have kept naming people, but that would put her to sleep. "They are prominent figures but also acquaintances. Most of the night will just be small talk, bullshit."

Her eyes stayed on Nadia. "Do you know her?"

"Yes. That's how I know her name and what she does for a living." I couldn't block the sarcasm from my voice.

She gave me a look full of attitude. "You know that's not what I was asking."

I stared at her blankly, having no idea what she meant. "Speak your mind because I can't read it."

"Did you sleep with her?" She turned blunt.

My eyes gently shifted back and forth as I looked into her gaze, surprised she would ask such a question. She didn't cross the line into my personal life and rarely expressed interest in it. "Because she's a model, you assume I slept with her?"

"Am I wrong?" she challenged.

She had me backed into a corner. "No."

She smiled slightly, as if in victory. "I figured."

"A bit of an assumption."

"You two have nothing in common in terms of business, so I doubt there was much talking going on." Her voice was borderline condescending, as if she judged me for having an affair with a beautiful woman.

It was almost as if she were jealous. "Since when do you care who I sleep with?"

"I never said I cared."

"Seems like you do."

*The Wolf and His Wife*

She stepped in close to me, looking up at me with eyes that matched the color of her dress. With her dark makeup, she looked more alluring than usual, so when she copped an attitude, it was somehow sexy. Now, she was so close, she could kiss me if she wanted to. And the closer she became, the more it seemed like her lips were about to touch mine. We hadn't kissed in public unless it was for a show. But this one would be genuine.

She moved in until her lips lightly pressed against mine, soft like rose petals. She kissed me as she held on to my arm for balance. The embrace was unexpected. She told me she didn't care who I slept with, but now she was kissing me like she wanted me to be hers.

It was ironic, considering Nadia wasn't nearly as beautiful as Arwen was.

But I would never tell my wife that.

She pulled back, a slight smile on her lips, like she knew a secret she would never share.

"Maverick DeVille." Franco Mancini approached us with his wife in tow. He was the owner of one of the most historic hotels in the city, a building that had been standing for hundreds of years. It'd been renovated but contained the same unique architecture that made it timeless. "Nice to see you, young man." He shook my hand.

"You as well, Franco. How's the hotel business?"

"No complaints," he said with a smile. "And the cheese business?"

"I have no complaints either." I smiled politely then introduced the woman beside me. "Franco, this is my wife,

Arwen." It was strange to say those words out loud, to introduce this woman as my wife. It started off as a ploy, but now it felt more real than ever. "Arwen, this is Franco Mancini. He owns the historic Le Sirense hotel here in Florence. And this is his wife, Carla."

"Nice to meet you both." She shook hands and allowed Franco to kiss her on the cheek. "I've seen your hotel, and it really is beautiful. Had lunch a couple of times."

"Thank you," Franco said. "It's in a lovely spot."

Carla smiled at both of us. "You two look really happy…definitely newlyweds."

My arm returned around Arwen's waist.

"Just like with cheese, you have great taste," Franco said. "I've known you for a long time, Maverick, and I've never seen you so happy. That's what happens when you fall in love… Same thing happened to me." He looked at his own wife. "And you'll be happy for a very long time."

---

"PLEASE SING SOMETHING, MRS. DEVILLE." Charles, the host of the party, practically begged my wife to serenade the room with her beautiful voice. "We would be so honored if you would sing us a song."

Even though Arwen was certain of her capabilities, she always looked shy when someone asked her to perform. She turned to me and silently asked permission.

I didn't want to let her go because she made this party more bearable, but I knew I couldn't hog her forever. "Just one song."

Charles took her by the wrist and pulled her away. "Thank you so much, Mrs. DeVille. I've seen you at the opera so many times…"

I stayed in the back with my glass of champagne, knowing people would swoop in for conversation any moment. We'd spent the evening talking to dozens of people, making small talk about the end of summer and work. Nadia didn't come near me because she spotted me with my wife and steered clear.

I still didn't know if Arwen was jealous or not.

Arwen sat at the piano with her chin tilted toward the keys. She avoided the gaze of everyone in the room as they stared at her and waited for her to play her song. She was used to attention, used to having an auditorium of people stare at her for hours, but these intimate gatherings softened her. Maybe it was because she played her own music instead of whatever the production provided for her. Perhaps it really was more intimate.

Her fingers stroked the keys, and the music filled the room. The tune was slightly quick, beautiful, and resonating, and she wove a vivid picture without singing a word. Then the words followed seconds later. "The kiss of a thorn, a painful sting. But the kiss of a petal, it becomes serene. Tough like hardwood and wise with rings. An ageless soul, too bitter to sing…" She captured the attention of every single person in the room. Even the waiters stopped serving because no one was interested in food or drink.

My eyes were focused on her, my dick hard in my slacks.

The second her voice turned poetic, I was stripped down to my masculine basics, reduced to a man that wanted the most beautiful woman in the room. The songs she sang were much better than the ones given to her at the opera. Her words were always so profound, but also cryptic.

"Damn, that woman can sing."

I stilled at the sound of his deep voice, recognizing it even though I'd only heard it a handful of times. With my glass in my hand, I slowly turned to the man who'd come to my side. At nearly seven feet with a maniacal gleam in his eyes, he stared at my wife like he had the same thoughts I did.

My heart picked up its pace, my fingers crushing my glass a little too hard. My eyes focused on the white teeth that were visible in his carnal smile. He was almost unrecognizable in his suit since he always wore casual clothes to our meetings. I hadn't expected him to appear, but when it came to money, it didn't matter how it was earned.

He finally turned his gaze on me, his eyes gray like steel. "I understand why you aren't eager to sell her."

Her music continued to play in the background. "The rock beneath my feet, the crutch for my knees, he's held my hand so sweet, never asked me to say please…"

I didn't carry a weapon, and even if I had, it would destroy my reputation if I'd drawn it at a party like this. All I could do was hold his gaze and watch him grin with joy, enjoying the fact that I was clearly caught off guard.

Kamikaze held a glass of champagne like he was a refined man who deserved to be there. "I'll make you a deal—"

"If you think you can just take her from me, you're mistaken.

*The Wolf and His Wife*

Cross me, and you cross all of my men. You walk onto a battlefield and start a war. We both know that's not something you want." I kept my voice low so the surrounding crowd wouldn't hear me, but they seemed more absorbed in Arwen's singing anyway.

He smiled slightly, like this was all some kind of joke. "I'm not going to take her from you, Maverick. Come on, I thought we had more respect for each other than that."

His words meant nothing because I knew this was still a threat—just veiled.

"I'm willing to offer a fair market value price for her. I'm not trying to rip you off, Maverick."

Maybe it was just business to him, but it was incredibly insulting to me. "She's not for sale—"

"Forty million." He took a drink of his champagne then wore a gloating smile.

Forty million was an astronomical amount for a human being. She wasn't the Duchess of Cambridge or the Queen of England. My father wanted her dead, and now this psychopath wanted to buy her like a cow for good steak. "No."

"Fifty."

"No."

"Sixty—"

"Not for fucking sale." I stepped closer to him, ready to break his jaw right there in the middle of the room. "How many times do I have to say it? You're gonna have to take her from me because I will never sell her."

He chuckled. "Wow...that must be good pussy."

He was clever to choose this party as the backdrop for our conversation—because I was paralyzed from doing anything.

"I'll cut you a deal. Keep in mind, I don't do this often. I'll buy her from you for a fair price, sixty million—but I'll give you a cut of the proceeds she earns through her lifetime. That's million-dollar checks every year until she gives out."

My jaw was so tight, it was liable to snap and break. The idea of Arwen being a slave to barbarians made me see so much red that I turned blind to all the other colors. All of this was happening because of her piece-of-shit father, and it made me lose all respect for his memory. I couldn't even get myself to say no because I was too pissed.

Kamikaze could read the answer on my face. "I'll take that as a no."

"She's not for sale. She'll never be for sale. Move on to something else, Kamikaze. I won't change my mind."

"I sure hope you do. I've always liked you, Maverick. I would really hate for things to get ugly..." He pivoted his body toward mine, looking me right in the eye. Arwen sang from the piano, her song slowly coming to a close. Kamikaze stared at me for a long time, his eyes shifting back and forth as he gauged my reaction. "And you know how ugly shit like this becomes."

---

ARWEN WAS CORNERED by her admirers, fielding questions about her singing and skills on the piano. Glasses of champagne kept being placed in her hand, and she kept drinking and drinking, bursting with laughter as her cheeks blushed with the alcohol.

I kept my arm around her waist so she wouldn't fall over and embarrass herself, but I wasn't really paying attention to her because my eyes continued to scan the room for signs of Kamikaze.

It seemed like he was gone.

I didn't want him anywhere near Arwen.

As the night continued, she got hammered. Laughing her heart out and making new friends, she was definitely the subject everyone would talk about for weeks to come. No one cared about me—just my beautiful and fascinating wife.

I finally pulled her aside when she'd had too much. "We should get going."

"Come on." She meant to pat her hand against my chest but hit my chin instead. "This is fun. You know which parties to hit."

"Nope. Party is over." I escorted her out of the house and to the valet at the end of the long pathway.

"Come on, live a little." She wobbled on her heels and almost tripped down one of the stairs. "Whoa...I thought I jumped out of an airplane for a second there."

I scooped her into my arms and carried her the rest of the way.

"Wow...you're so strong." She wrapped her arms around my neck and kissed me on the neck.

I carried her to the car and got her into the passenger seat. I had to buckle her safety belt because even that was too hard for her. Then I drove home, listening to her mumble about nonsense in the seat beside me. Then she started to hum... but that was actually nice.

When we got home, I carried her inside and up the stairs. When we reached the second floor, I turned to carry her to her bedroom.

"No...I want to sleep with you," she whispered in my ear, her melodic voice innately seductive.

I didn't want to sleep with a drunk woman, but maybe keeping her with me was smart. I wouldn't want her to choke on her own vomit and die. The only way to make sure she lasted through the night was if I was beside her the entire time.

I turned around and carried her to my bedroom.

She was light in my arms and still beautiful with smeared makeup, and I felt lucky this woman came home with me every night. Every man in that room wanted her, married or not. But I was the one who got to have her. Kamikaze wanted her more because it was obvious how alluring she was, how much a man would pay to have her for the night.

The thought made me sick to my stomach, so I stopped thinking about it.

I set her on the bed with her legs dangling over the edge. I loosened the straps of her heels then pushed them off so her feet could finally relax.

She lay there, her eyes closed like she was dead tired.

I turned her over and found the zipper at the back of her dress. I tugged it open and loosened the dress so I could pull it down her body toward her hips.

When her tits popped out, her eyes opened. Firm and round with cute nipples, her tits pointed straight up as she shook her hips to get herself out of the gown. She watched me, studying the way I stared at her body without shame.

I got the material to her ankles then tossed it over the chair.

When I came back to her, she already had pushed her thong off, leaving her completely naked on my bed. She spread her legs when I came near, beckoning me to stand between her thighs and fuck her.

I didn't care that she was drunk. She was my wife, and I could fuck her whenever I wanted. My palm pressed against her flat tummy, and I slid my hand up between her voluptuous tits. I touched her warm cleavage and watched her suck in a deep breath, filled with desire. My eyes worshiped her perfect figure, from her slender stomach to her nice pussy.

She grabbed my hips and tugged on me, wanting me to lean over her so she could kiss me.

I fell forward and held my body up with my arms, my lips just inches from hers.

With parted lips and lazy eyes, she looked at me like she wanted me to stick it to her good. "You're the only man I want to go home with..." Her palms planted against my chest, and she pressed her lips to mine. She kissed me slowly but passionately, giving me her eager tongue as her fingers loosened my tie and unbuttoned my shirt. She pushed my shirt off my shoulders then moved to my slacks. The belt came off and the zipper was undone. "Now I know what it really means to be with a man…"

My cock nearly exploded in my boxers because this felt like a dream. I'd done dirty talk with beautiful women, but I'd never experienced something like this…when the most desirable woman in the world made me feel like the most desirable man.

I pulled away in my eagerness and dropped my boxers. A condom was on my shaft in seconds, and then I grabbed her hips and dragged her to the edge of the bed. I was prepared to fuck her deep and hard, to sheathe my dick until only my balls hung out.

I pushed my head inside her and slowly made my entrance, gliding through the slickness she'd already produced. She was so wet for me…matching the words she whispered to me. I closed my eyes as I moved all the way into her, buried inside the slit of heaven.

She gripped my wrists and moaned, her head rolling back with her plump lips wide apart.

I lowered my body on top of hers so I could kiss her again, feel her lips while my dick treasured her cunt. Even through the condom, I could feel her so intimately, feel how wet and tight she was.

Her fingers moved into my hair, and she gasped against my mouth, "Yes…I was jealous."

I rested my forehead against hers and felt my dick twitch.

"Very jealous."

## 7

## ARWEN

"More coffee?" Abigail stood with the stainless-steel pitcher.

My fingertips rested against my temple as I tried to combat the migraine that throbbed in my head. The pulse was so powerful, and the strongest cup of coffee in the world couldn't change that. I pushed my mug closer to her anyway. "Please."

She poured the coffee, the liquid the same color as Maverick's eyes.

"Thank you."

"Long night, huh?"

"Yeah...something like that."

Abigail gave me a non-judgmental smile. "A big meal always gets me back on my feet."

I'd already thrown up, so my stomach was empty. I should probably put some food in it. "Good advice."

She walked away.

I grabbed my fork and dug into my salad, my eyes squinting in the afternoon sunlight. Fall had reached Tuscany, but it would still be warm for a few months. When the cold arrived, the charm would disappear.

Minutes later, Maverick joined me. In a t-shirt and jeans, he looked thoroughly rested, like he'd slept better than he ever had. He skipped the coffee because he'd already had some that morning and poured himself a glass of iced tea instead.

Jealous, I stared at him.

He grabbed his fork and dug into his salad, eating across from me like it was a normal day. He felt amazing, and I felt like shit. "Don't drink so much next time."

"I can't turn down good champagne…"

"You drank more than just champagne," he teased. "You were downing wine and hard liquor throughout the night."

I couldn't remember that. "No wonder I feel like shit…"

He drank his iced tea and looked at me. "Remember much of it?"

"I remember playing the piano. Was I any good?" I remembered singing one of my songs. That was the last clear memory I possessed. Everything turned dark after that.

He rolled his eyes like it was a stupid question. "You were phenomenal. Everyone fell in love with you…like they always do."

"No wonder I drank so much. I hope I didn't embarrass you."

"No. In fact, you make me look good." He kept eating his lunch, stabbing the tomatoes and mozzarella with his fork before placing them into his mouth. The meals Abigail gave him were always low in carbs and high in protein. It was the only way he could keep a fit body like that. He suddenly stopped eating and rolled his left shoulder like it was sore. He released a quiet sigh as he rubbed the area.

"Are you alright?"

"Yeah." He dropped his hand and kept eating. "It hasn't healed all the way. Gets sore from time to time."

I left my chair and walked around the table behind him. My hands pressed into the back of his shoulder, and I dug into the area, gently massaging the area until I located the tightness. His muscles were full of knots, and I gently rolled them until they were smooth.

Maverick was tense at first, but his muscles slowly relaxed, and he gave in to the goodness of the massage. He stopped eating and just sat there, enjoying the way my fingers relieved the unwanted pressure.

I rubbed his back for a few minutes, letting him relax completely before I pulled my fingers away. When I returned to my chair, I saw the relaxed look in his eyes, like he could fall asleep right at the table. "Thanks…"

"Sure."

He leaned forward again and dug his fork into his lunch. "I was going to visit my sister tonight. Would you like to come?"

I'd asked to see her before, but it didn't seem like he was interested in connecting us. He'd obviously had a change of heart. "Yeah, I'd love to." I didn't know anything about his sister, but if she was a kind person, unlike his father, I definitely wanted to meet her. I was sick of the darkness that surrounded the DeVille family members.

"Alright. Hopefully, you have enough time to sober up before that happens."

"I just need another cup of coffee…and maybe a nap."

---

THE REHAB CENTER was in Florence. In a large building just a couple blocks from the opera house, the facility was a spacious and luxurious space that allowed its residents to have a safe place to heal. It felt like a resort more than a place to keep people confined. The staff was extremely helpful. The floors were a beautiful hardwood, and the walls were warm gray with white trim. We entered the dining area that more closely resembled a five-star restaurant than a cafeteria.

When we approached the booth, she was already sitting there. With the same dark hair, brown eyes, and olive-colored skin of my husband, she looked exactly like a DeVille. But one thing set her apart from Maverick and her father.

This girl could actually smile.

Her eyes lit up when she saw her brother. They became even brighter when she saw me. "You actually brought her. Good, I was afraid you would lock her in a closet and never let her see the sky."

"I'm not a monster." Maverick scooted into the booth without embracing her with affection.

I took the seat beside him. "It's nice to meet you, Lily. Maverick has mentioned you a few times. I didn't even know he had a sister until I asked him directly."

"He's embarrassed of me." She admitted. "But that's okay. I'm embarrassed of him too."

I definitely liked her more than Caspian. She was in rehab because she was struggling, but she knew how to take a joke and be cheerful. Maverick and his father were brooding all the time, day and night.

"You have any siblings?" she asked.

"No." I shook my head. "Only child." As a result, I was the only living person left of my family lineage. Maybe having a sibling would have made losing my father a little easier.

"You're super pretty," she blurted. "Maverick showed me a picture, but it didn't do you justice, not that you don't photograph well, of course."

"Oh...thanks. You are too."

"So, what's new with you guys?"

Maverick wasn't talkative, so he barely said a few sentences. "Just working a lot."

"And Father?" she asked. "How's he?"

Maverick only gave a shrug.

Lily watched him for a long time before she looked at me. "You probably know that our father is an asshole, right?"

"Yeah…he's a little cold."

"A little?" she asked with a laugh. "That guy is something else. Maverick told me you saved those two girls. I know it's not my place to give an opinion, but I think you did the right thing."

That meant the world to me. "Thanks…"

"It's easy to hate my father because of his behavior, but it's hard for me to forget how he used to be. As difficult as it is to believe, he used to be a great father. He would take us to the park, swim with us in the backyard, and spend a lot of time with us. But as time goes on, Maverick and I understand he's not that man anymore…and he probably never will be again."

That must be the hardest part, hating someone when they used to be so good. "I'm sorry. I can't imagine how hard it is for both of you." I saw the way Maverick carried the weight every single day. It always bothered him, always haunted him.

Maverick spoke up again. "He told me to kill Arwen."

Lily cocked an eyebrow. "What?"

"He told me to kill her since she released those girls. I refused. Now we're enemies…"

Lily dragged her hands down her face then looked at the table. "Jesus, this is a nightmare."

"I'm sorry." I hadn't meant for this to happen, but I felt like I should apologize.

"It's not your fault," she said with a sigh. "He's lost his mind… He lost it a long time ago."

"I'm still sorry..." I saw the way it affected both of them. They were grown adults, but having an unhinged father was devastating to both of them. "You guys don't deserve this. I wish there were a way to make him see reason." He threatened to hurt his own son all the time and hadn't visited his daughter once in rehab. The man clearly didn't care. Now he wanted to kill me...which was enough burden for Maverick to carry.

"He can't see reason," Maverick said coldly. "And he never will."

---

When we finished dinner, Maverick excused himself to wash his hands in the bathroom.

That left Lily and me alone at the table.

"Is my brother treating you right? And don't worry, you can answer honestly. I won't tell him anything you say."

Sometimes he could be a dick, but for the most part, he was wonderful. "Yes...he's a good man." He made sure I got home after a night of drinking, and when some guy didn't know when to back off, he took care of it. He took care of me in so many ways. "He's rough around the edges, a little heartless at times, but I wouldn't change anything about him."

She kept her fingers around her glass as she watched me. "He told me he asked for a divorce when everything went down. Said you betrayed his trust. But the fact that he trusted you to begin with was interesting. That was how I knew you were special...because you are special."

She was definitely the kinder sibling, the observant one who could see past the hostility to the goodness underneath. "He and I have a good relationship. In the beginning, it was hard for us because neither one of us wanted to get married... especially to someone we didn't know. But we've become friends...started to trust each other. I lost my father and have felt so low, but he's always there for me. Sometimes, he pisses me off, but he always makes up for it."

She smiled. "It seems like my brother is more than just a friend to you."

"Of course. He's my husband." Now I used that term literally because it was the best way to describe our relationship. That was exactly what we were—husband and wife. We were friends; we were lovers. We worked together and supported each other.

She continued to smile. "I know he cares about you. He doesn't actually say those words or give anything away...but he does."

I'd known that for a long time. "I know this is a lot to ask, but do you think you could help me with something?"

"With Maverick?" she asked with a slight laugh. "That guy is so stubborn... I don't think there's anything I can do. You're the only one who has any effect on him."

She had a lot more effect than she realized. "The reason why Maverick and your father are at odds is because of me... and I want to fix that."

"I don't see how you can."

"Maybe if I could get him alone, we could talk about it...and I could make him understand how he's treating Maverick, how he's lost sight of the things that matter. I don't just want to convince him to drop his vendetta against me. I also want him to be better to both of you."

Lily stared at me like I was crazy. "The second you're in a room with him, he'll kill you. That plan is a terrible idea. Stay away from him."

"The same thought crossed my mind. If I showed up on his doorstep, he'd probably shoot me."

"Good…I'm glad you aren't being stupid."

"But if you asked him to come down here to see you…I would be safe." He wouldn't bring a gun into the building, and there would be too many witnesses around. He couldn't sit across the table from me then choke me with his bare hands. It would give us plenty of time to talk, under the banner of truce.

Now Lily was even more shocked. "I don't know…"

"It's harmless. What could possibly go wrong?"

"I don't know, but Maverick says nothing but bad things about him now."

"They're all true." Every single one of them. "But I have to try. Maverick can't reason with him…you can't reason with him. Maybe if I talked about my relationship with my father, it would help him understand how he's acting."

She shook her head. "Maverick would be pissed at me…"

"But you're his sister, so he'll forgive you. Besides, what if this works? What if this chips at his armor a little bit? What if this helps repair the relationship? If we don't start to reverse the damage now, it'll just get worse and worse until it's beyond fixing. Please help me, Lily. It's just one conversation."

She glanced at the bathroom, checking for her brother. "I don't want to put you in danger."

"What's he going to do to me here?" I challenged.

"I don't know…but I like you. I don't want anything bad to happen to you."

"It won't. And this means a lot to me. If I could fix this, Maverick would have what he wants most in this world…his family." It was all I wanted for him, for him to feel loved. He was unable to take a compliment, to accept any kind of goodness because he didn't feel like he deserved it. He was a giver—not a receiver. But I didn't want him to live his entire life that way. "He's coming back… Please say yes."

Lily relaxed her shoulders as she gave in. "Alright…I'll do it."

# 8

# MAVERICK

Arwen was at the opera for the evening, so I went out for a drink with Kent. The bar was quiet on a Wednesday night, a few girls standing at the bar, while the booths were full of people catching up.

With a scotch in my hand and shoulders full of fatigue after a long day at the office, I stared into the amber liquid and remembered the conversation I'd had with my sister last night. On the surface, she seemed perfectly normal, as if she didn't struggle to keep her hands off booze and more sinister substances. But she wouldn't still be there if she felt well enough to walk away. She had an empty apartment waiting for her, a whole life that needed to be lived.

Kent rambled on about shit that happened at work. "The guy wouldn't pay, and I nearly pulled my knife on him…but then sense hit him hard in the skull." He drank from his glass then glanced at the two women in the corner. He was in a gray blazer with black jeans, his hair dark like mine. He was easy to pick up women with because he had a lot to offer.

I kept looking into my glass, my mind a million miles away.

Kent kept looking at the women. "I wouldn't mind a blow job from one of them, but that's about it."

I hadn't even looked at them.

Kent turned back to me when I didn't say anything. "Something on your mind?"

"My sister is still in rehab, and my father wants to kill me… I've got a lot on my mind."

"Then kill him first. There's your solution."

I despised my father for a lot of reasons, but the idea of killing him didn't sit right with me. In my twisted brain, I still believed he could come back from this dark place… somehow. Even if he really would kill me if he had the chance, I wasn't sure if I could do the same to him. I didn't possess much compassion, but it felt inherently wrong to murder my own kin. "That's not the solution I want."

"Then try talking to him."

"He won't listen."

"Then we're back to square one…kill him."

That seemed to be my only alternative.

"And he wants to kill your wife too?"

He wasn't the only one. "He mainly wants her dead… He'd probably spare me if I didn't get in his way."

"Dude, your dad is a psychopath."

"I know."

He shook his head and took another drink. "I understand he lost his wife, but how does someone flip a switch like that?"

That was the reason my finger didn't squeeze the trigger. I still remembered the kind man he used to be like it was yesterday…because it really wasn't that long ago. Lily and I used to come over every Sunday for dinner. My father and I would talk about work or sports, and Lily and my mother would bake cookies in the kitchen after work. I never really appreciated it until it was gone. Now, all the members of my family had disappeared…and I only had Arwen. She carried my last name and seemed loyal to me, so I guess she was family.

"I don't know what to tell you, Maverick. There's no easy solution. But letting it continue until he makes a move is no solution either…unless you don't care if he kills your wife."

Killing my wife would solve all of my problems—every single one. But she was the one thing that was worth protecting. She'd become my friend, my ally. She was the star of every party I took her to…and the bigger star in my bed. She was a good person and didn't deserve the wrath of those evil men, and that meant I had to protect her. "I do care."

Kent ran his fingers along the rim of his glass. "How's that going?"

"What?"

"You know what."

I didn't share any details about our relationship because it felt wrong. I wanted to protect her privacy. She was also my wife...and I didn't want to talk about fucking her to someone else. "It's fine."

"Fine?" he asked. "I figured it would be more than fine with a woman like that."

I took a long drink. "Let's talk about something else."

Kent smiled slightly. "Alright." He turned back to the women at the bar. "You want the brunette, and I get the blonde?" He'd just said he didn't find them that attractive, but we weren't picky on nights like this. It was obviously a test, to see exactly where I stood.

I glanced at them, thoroughly unimpressed. The more my eyes wandered to the tail in this city, the more I realized how special my wife was. She had legs for days, tits perfect for sucking, and she was an incredible lover. Made everyone seem plain by comparison.

"Maverick?" Kent pressed me into an answer.

I took another drink and let the booze burn my throat. "Sure."

---

I WALKED in the door late that night and headed to the kitchen. I grabbed a glass from the pantry and filled it with water. After all the booze I'd had, I needed something pure. I let the water drip down my throat and cleanse the alcohol from my blood.

Abigail revealed herself from the other side of the room, her hair in a braid with pajamas on her body. She could be dead asleep, but if she knew someone was in the kitchen, her eyes popped wide open. "Long night?"

I finished my glass of water then left it on the counter next to the sink. "A bit."

"Can I make you something?"

"No. Not hungry." I'd sat at the bar and listened to the brunette drone on about whatever she was talking about. When she grabbed my thigh, I pulled away. When she tried to kiss me, I rejected her on instinct. Kent went home with the blonde, and I left the bar alone.

Abigail kept watching me. "Arwen came home not too long ago. She's probably still awake."

"What's that supposed to mean?" Abigail knew my marriage was bogus. It was just an arrangement to get what I wanted—what my father wanted. But Arwen had obviously charmed Abigail just like she did with everyone else.

"It's rare for you to come home alone with scotch on your breath…that's all."

Only Abigail could talk to me like that. Anyone else would be fired. But I needed her way too much to ever let her go, so she got away with pretty much everything. "Just wasn't my night."

"Or maybe it was." With a knowing look in her eyes, she gave me a smile. Then she walked out of the kitchen to let me think about what she'd just said.

It didn't take me long to ponder her meaning. I came home alone because I wanted to be alone. If I hadn't found a woman I liked at that bar, I could have just gone to another.

But the urge to find a woman for the night had disappeared. Why search for something you already had?

I left the kitchen and headed upstairs to the second landing. When I reached the top, I ran into Arwen.

In a nightdress with her face washed clean of makeup, she stilled next to the banister, clearly surprised to bump into me on her journey. Her eyes took me in with her guard up, but slowly, she turned docile. "You're home late."

"I was out with Kent."

"Yeah…I can smell the scotch from here."

"I always smell like scotch."

She smiled slightly. "And you're alone… That's unusual."

I wanted to tell her that I didn't find anyone I liked, that I searched but was unable to find anyone that interested me. But that would be a lie, and I didn't have the energy to weave a bullshit story. The reason I was alone was because I wanted to be alone. She knew it…I knew it. "What are you doing?"

"Going to the kitchen."

"Thirsty?"

"No…just wanted a snack. I never eat before a performance because I want to look as slim as possible, but then I'm so hungry afterward."

I had no idea why, but I found that cute. "Want me to make you something?"

"No," she said with a laugh. "I was just going to rummage through the fridge until I found something good."

"I'll come with you. I could use a snack too."

We returned to the kitchen, and she opened the fridge and let the light fill the dark room. "Hmm...there's lots of options here." Her nightdress was short and showed her sexy legs in the light from the refrigerator. With one hand on her hip and her head tilted to the side, she examined the contents. "Leftover ravioli...that looks pretty good."

Abigail probably knew we'd returned to the kitchen, but she didn't appear to offer to cook anything so she could leave us alone. I watched Arwen pull out the container and set it on the counter. "Want to split it?"

I wasn't hungry. "Sure."

She put it in the microwave for a minute before she pulled it out again. She set it on the counter and grabbed two forks. She put one ravioli into her mouth and moaned like she hadn't eaten in weeks. "Cheese ravioli...so good."

I put one in my mouth, unimpressed because I was used to Abigail's culinary perfection. "How was the opera?"

"Good. Uneventful." She kept eating, standing with me at the counter. "How was Kent?"

"Good. Uneventful."

She chuckled. "I doubt you would spend so much time with him if that were the case."

"We talked about my father...shit like that." Sometimes, we had a good time. Sometimes, we talked about serious stuff.

"That sounds like a deep conversation."

"He told me I should kill my father...but I can't do it." I set my fork down and leaned against the counter as I watched her continue to eat. I loved the way her plump lips parted as she slipped the ravioli inside. Her mouth was sexy, regardless of what she did with it.

"There's still hope."

I shook my head. "I really don't think there is." My father had threatened to kill me several times now, even though once was already enough. "But it's hard for me to forget that he's my father…the person who taught me to ride a bike and become a man. I have to remember that's not who he is anymore, but there's something deep inside me that believes he might change."

"He might…"

I shook my head again. "It's not gonna happen."

She took another bite then watched me with sad eyes. Even without makeup, she was stunning. With that thick hair and bright eyes, she always had the appearance of a doll. She set her fork down and returned the lid to the container. "I'm sorry…" She moved in front of me and placed her hands on my chest. "You don't deserve to go through this… I wish I could fix it." Her eyes looked at her hands against my chest, her fingertips feeling my hard torso through my shirt. She slowly lifted her chin to meet my gaze, her eyes still sympathetic.

Despite all the times I was a dick to her, she still cared about me. She felt my pain, carried my burden. She needed me when times got tough for her, but she always reciprocated that support. Her words seemed so genuine, I could actually feel it in my heart.

She continued to watch me, looking like a dream as the moonlight entered through the windows. Her eyes sparkled, no matter what, even if there wasn't a single light shining from the ceiling. Her eyes were focused on me, two diamonds set in a beautiful face.

My hands moved around her waist, and I pulled her closer to me, bringing our foreheads together. I squeezed tighter, feeling her petiteness through the thin silk of her dress. I could feel the contours of her body so easily, like there was nothing separating us at all.

She closed her eyes and moved her hands to my arms, her fingertips gripping my bare skin. Her breathing picked up like she knew exactly what was going to happen next.

I was hard in my jeans, hard for the first time that day. The women at the bar did nothing for me, not like this woman did. Her beauty was unparalleled, her sexiness was scorching. My hands slid to her perfect ass, and I squeezed it.

She moaned because she loved it when I did that. She loved it when my manly hands squeezed her so tight.

My fingers bunched up the material of her dress until her ass poked out of the silk. In just a simple white thong, her creamy skin always looked so delicious. My mouth moved to hers, and I planted a gentle kiss on her lips, my cock stirring in my jeans the second we made contact.

She breathed hard into my mouth, like it was the first time we'd ever kissed.

My hand slid into her hair, and I kissed her in my kitchen, kissed her like we were alone in my bedroom. My mouth turned aggressive instantly, devouring her lips like they were my favorite dessert. My other hand moved down her ass and between her legs, my fingertips finding her clit through her panties. I rubbed the area hard, making her gasp in my mouth when her nerves were set on fire.

I could feel the moisture on my fingertips already.

"Maverick…" Her hands moved under my shirt and felt my chiseled physique, her fingers sliding into the grooves of my abs. She wanted me so much, was so undeniably attracted to me. She told me I was the best she'd ever had, that I was a real man.

That was a compliment coming from a woman like her.

She undid my jeans and let them slide to the floor before she pulled my shirt over my head. She pulled off her own panties next but left her silky dress in place.

I lifted her onto the kitchen counter and moved between her thighs, my lips still kissing hers. My cock hung in the air, dripping wet and throbbing. I'd been depressed just moments ago, but now I was more aroused than I'd ever been. My balls were so tight with eagerness.

I grabbed a condom from my pocket and rolled it down to my base.

Her arms hooked around my neck, and she breathed against my mouth as she felt me slowly inch inside her. My large head stretched her apart as it entered her tightness. Then it sank farther and farther until I was balls deep.

She sighed into my mouth, her body full of a big dick. "Yes…"

I held on to her ass and scooped her into my arms so I could pound into her. I'd never fucked a woman in my kitchen, but it was better than any fantasy I could have dreamed of. The most beautiful woman in the world was taking me, enjoying me, and asking for more.

I watched her stunning reaction, watched her lips part with a sexy moan that sounded like the loveliest music. Her pussy was so fucking wet that I wished this piece of latex weren't separating us. I wished I could feel her skin-to-skin, come deep inside her, and watch it drip between her thighs.

She lay back against the counter and lifted up her dress so I could see her tits.

I grabbed her hips and pulled her into me as my hips thrust to slide farther inside her. Her tits shook with every push, her nipples hard and sexy. I closed my eyes because it felt so good to fuck this woman. Anywhere, anytime, it was the best I'd ever had. My balls tightened toward my body as I prepared to explode with arousal, to fill her cunt with everything I had. Her moans bounced off the tiles and the hard surfaces, amplifying its volume. Her hands latched on to my wrists, and she bit her lips as she tried to stop herself from screaming.

Why would I want someone else when I could have this?

When I could have my wife?

# 9
## ARWEN

With legs made of lead and a rapid heartbeat that wouldn't slow down, I rounded the corner to the rehab center and found Caspian sitting in one of the booths. A hot cup of coffee sat in front of him, the rising steam visible this far away. An obscure painting was on the wall, and most of the dining area was empty with the exception of a few guests.

There he was…my father-in-law.

His hands were joined together in his lap, and he stared straight ahead, his shoulders wide and his eyes unblinking. He had dark hair like his son, though there were sprinkles of gray within the locks. But his eyes were exactly the same, pools of espresso. His facial structure was similar to his son's, innately masculine. Maverick must have inherited his softer features from his mother, making him so handsome.

There was still time to turn around and call the whole thing off.

But seeing him there gave me some hope. Lily had called and asked him to come…and he did.

He wasn't completely heartless after all.

I entered the dining room and caught his attention. His eyes flicked to me, and with a predatory gaze, he watched me approach his table. Just like Maverick, he never gave the impression he was surprised or caught off guard. Like he'd been expecting me the entire time, he was calm.

I approached the table, my heart beating like a drum. I slid into the booth and sat across from him, his bold eyes boring into mine as if they could cut right through me. His wrath was palpable, his desire for murder practically audible. Maverick was nowhere nearby. He was probably at the office at the house, nowhere close enough to help me. I suddenly felt like an unguarded sheep, not nearly as secure as I was when my wolf was keeping his eyes on the perimeter. I was really on my own…and I felt it.

Caspian stared at me with unblinking eyes. He took in my features with a coldness that felt like ice. He slowly moved his hands to the surface of the table, showing me that he didn't have a weapon in hand. He leaned forward slightly, trying to intimidate me with his glare.

I got the attention of the waitress. "May I get a coffee?"

Caspian's glare deepened at the way I'd brushed him off.

The hot mug was placed in front of me.

Just to be obnoxious, I took a drink.

Caspian didn't move.

I set the mug down and regarded him again, coldly but still playful.

"You're a stupid girl. My son is doing everything he can to protect you, and you're sneaking around behind his back. He should kill you for that kind of disobedience."

"Disobedience?" I cocked an eyebrow. "I'm a woman—not a dog."

"You're a bitch if you ask me."

Just when I thought this man couldn't get worse, he raised the bar. "I didn't arrange this meeting so you could insult me. I didn't arrange it so I could insult you either—even though I should."

"Then what do you want? Other than a death wish?"

I wanted him to be a good person, but that didn't seem possible. "First of all, I wanted to say I'm so sorry about your wife…"

The apology tugged at his iciness very slightly. He couldn't hide the surprise from spreading across his face—not this time. He was tense and prepared for an attack or an insult. Instead, he got sympathy.

"Maverick tells me she was a wonderful person and mother… I'm sorry that all of you had to lose her. She didn't deserve what happened to her, and I'm glad Ramon died a terrible death."

Now his face was stoic. "If you really meant that, you wouldn't have interfered."

"I do mean it. But I don't think his wife and daughter deserved the same fate."

"We can argue about this all day, but I won't change my mind. He raped and killed my wife. I should have done the same to his."

"Torturing and killing him was sufficient."

"Not to the man who was married to her," he said coldly. "Not to the man who raised a family with her, who planned to grow old with her and die with her. How dare you tell me what kind of justice I deserve! You're a stupid girl who doesn't know a damn thing." His hands shook slightly as he fought the fury from taking over his body. His mind was so deeply enmeshed in his sick need for violence that he couldn't think clearly at all.

"My father did some shady things I had nothing to do with. Now some very bad men want to punish me for his crimes. I know how it feels to be the innocent person who's guilty by association. I know how it feels to be scared because of something you didn't even do. I know how those women felt…because I am those women."

His rage didn't dissipate—not at all.

"When I took them out of the barn, I kept Ramon in place. It would have been wrong for me to free him because he deserved the punishment you set for him. He even agreed. He was just grateful I'd saved his girls that he stayed voluntarily."

"Which makes your crime even worse," he whispered. "Your father asked me for a favor, and I saved your ass. I gave my son to you, a man strong enough to keep the bastards away. This is how you repay me?"

"Let's not forget we made a deal—no one did any favors."

"Giving you a good husband is much better than giving me details about Ramon."

"But you accepted that offer and forced your son to marry a stranger."

He cocked his head to the side, his eyes narrowed. "I don't think my son has any complaints about that anymore."

I certainly didn't. I came home to a man I respected and admired. I came home to a man I wanted to sleep with every night. He took care of me, kept me safe, gave me whatever I wanted. I'd hated my situation in the beginning—but now I knew I'd hit the jackpot. "Nor do I."

"I assumed. No other reason for you to risk your neck like this."

I was putting myself in danger, but the risk had been worth it. My interest wasn't just in saving my neck. It was giving Maverick what he deserved. "Your son and daughter need you, Caspian. You've turned into a demon since you lost your wife. They need the man you used to be... They need a father."

"My children are both adults. They don't need me anymore."

"That's where you're wrong," I whispered. "I needed my father up until the day he died...and I still need him now. You need to drop these hostilities with Maverick and treat him with affection and respect."

"I will do so when he deserves it." He kept his voice even, only his tone changing with his passion. To any onlooker in the room, we probably looked a father and daughter catching up over warm cups of coffee. In reality, a storm was building.

"He's your son—he deserved it from the day he was born."

His dark eyes shifted back and forth slightly as he looked into mine. "Maverick has forgotten where his loyalties lie. I asked him to kill you, and he refused. He's made it clear that a nice ass is more important than family."

"I'm not a nice ass…" I was so much more than that. Maverick wouldn't wage a war with his father over sex. "Your mind is unhinged, and you aren't thinking clearly. You threatened to kill him several times before this happened—"

"To straighten him out. He's grown too soft for my taste."

This moment made me appreciate my father even more. He was wrong to make his mistakes, but he always loved me. He was always good to me. "Maverick tells me that you used to be different when your wife was still here. You were a good man…a good father. He hopes that version of you will come back someday."

It was the first time he didn't have a reply. He lifted his mug and brought it to his lips for a drink, keeping his eyes on me.

This meeting was a waste after all.

"If Maverick wants to repair his relationship with me, then he needs to put a bullet between your eyes and leave your body in a ditch. Then we can talk."

"What good will that accomplish?"

"Justice—for me."

"I didn't hurt your wife. I had nothing to do with it."

"You had everything to do with it when you took those girls away from me." He was singular in his thoughts, only focusing on one thing to the exclusion of all else.

"Would you have felt any better if you'd raped and murdered them?" I questioned. "Would it really have made all that much of a difference? Would the reality of her death be less bitter to swallow?"

His eyes began to narrow once more. "Yes."

"Liar." My hostility began to rise. "It would have made no difference. I'm sorry that your wife is dead, Caspian. But she is dead. Killing more people won't bring her back. Spilled blood won't make you sleep better at night. If you want to honor her memory, keep your family together. You've been doing a terrible job so far."

His hands came together, and his fingers tightened forcefully.

"You need to let this go. You need to focus on the family you have left. Maverick won't say this to your face, but he's hurt… He's hurt that things have gotten this bad. He misses having a father. He misses spending time with his family on Sundays. Now all he has is a father who is only disappointed in him. He has a father who doesn't care that his sister is in rehab—"

"Don't sit there and tell me my faults. Your father was a worthless scumbag who didn't give a damn about you. If he had, he wouldn't have pissed away every penny he had so his daughter would be left destitute and married off to a stranger. Judge me all you want, but I can do the same to you."

"I'm not judging you—"

"You are judging me—and I don't like it." He rose to his feet and got out of the booth. "Your little ploy worked this time, but if I see you again, I won't hesitate to put a bullet in that pretty mouth of yours."

My good intentions evaporated in my face, and I seemed to have made everything worse, not better. I'd made Caspian feel insulted, and I only boiled his rage at a higher temperature. "I want my husband to have his father. Forget about me…and think about him."

He stayed near the table as he looked down at me. "You're the wedge between us. You're the reason my wife didn't get the justice she deserved. If you want to make this right, if you want your husband to have some kind of relationship with his father, then you'll do the right thing."

"Even if the right thing would devastate him?" I challenged. "I'm the best thing that's ever happened to your son…and he's the best thing that's ever happened to me. Tearing us apart would accomplish nothing. Your son's happiness should be the most important thing to you."

"No," he said coldly. "My wife's memory is the most important thing to me—not the opinion of a whore."

---

THE CURTAINS FELL, and I headed backstage to dab at the sweat that marked my forehead. I pulled the pins out of my hair and let it come loose from my scalp. People gave their congratulations as they passed by on their way to their stations.

I looked in the mirror and wiped off the bright lipstick with a tissue. I tore off the fake eyelashes too. As more pieces of my stage makeup came off, I started to look like myself, like the person I actually knew.

The second I stopped hustling, I thought about my conversation with Caspian yesterday.

Nothing had changed.

If anything, that man wanted to kill me even more.

I didn't risk my neck to save my own ass. I wanted to fix the broken relationship between father and son, to give Maverick what he wanted more than anything. But it blew up in my face…because Caspian was the biggest asshole on the planet.

I felt a presence in my vanity mirror, a dark expression that followed me everywhere I went, even in my dreams. My gaze lifted, and I spotted the espresso-colored eyes staring into mine. With a slight smirk on his handsome face, he was delighted to catch a glimpse of me when I hadn't noticed.

My heart raced as I stared at Maverick, the butterflies soaring in my stomach and my blood running hot. He made me feel weak in the knees but strong everywhere else. He made my breath hitch slightly, like I didn't get quite enough air with every single breath. My hands pushed against the vanity as I rose to my feet, feeling the faint smile form on my lips as I met his gaze.

Even in heels, he was still taller than me. With that dark hair and those dark eyes, he was lethal in his charm. When he wore a black suit, it only made him more appealing. His smile widened as he stepped toward me, his arms circling my petite waist as he pulled me into his chest. My husband held me tightly then kissed me.

Kissed me good.

His hand gave my ass a gentle squeeze before he pulled away.

I liked it when he did that—even in public.

"You were great, Sheep."

"Thank you..."

He stepped to the side and revealed his friend Kent. "You remember Kent. You met a couple of months ago."

"Yes, I remember." We hadn't talked much, but I remember him sitting across the table, his lips locked with a pretty girl's. He was Maverick's height with the same level of attractiveness—even though he wasn't my type. "Nice to see you again."

"You too." He smiled before he leaned in and kissed me on the cheek. "Damn, you can sing. It's incredible that such a small woman can make such loud music. You must be tired after singing for two hours."

"I usually have some lemon and water after a night like that, but I love every minute of it." I felt Maverick come to my side and wrap his arm around my waist, playing the dutiful husband in the public eye. But his affection didn't feel forced or fake. Now it felt natural...like he wanted to hold me at his side.

"Do what you love and never work a day in your life, huh?"

Kent stood with his hands in his pockets, glancing at the pretty girls as they walked by. He turned his attention back to me. "Maverick and I were going out for drinks but decided to stop by and see the show."

Last time Maverick went to a bar, he came home alone. I felt relieved when there wasn't another woman on his arm. It'd been a while since he'd brought a stranger home, and I'd gotten used to the exclusivity. I liked it just being us…no one else. But if he was going out for drinks tonight, then maybe our exclusivity had come to an end. "That's nice. Thanks for stopping by."

"Want to come with us?" Maverick tilted his gaze down so he could look at me, his cologne fragrant. It immediately reminded me of sex, when the sweat from his body made it release from his pores. "We can watch Kent make an idiot out of himself."

"I never make an idiot out of myself," Kent argued. "I always go home with someone."

"But you get slapped too," Maverick teased.

Kent rolled his eyes. "That happened one time. I was a little drunk and tired, and I just wanted to get to the point."

"What does that mean?" I asked.

Maverick turned to me. "He walked up to a woman and, point-blank, asked if she wanted to come over to fuck. Didn't buy her a drink or even ask her name."

Kent sighed. "Like I said, I was tired…"

I could understand why that would be a turn-off for any woman. It was impersonal and rude. "I'm sure it would work if you did it..." If I saw Maverick across the room, I'd do anything to get him to come home with me. I'd be the one buying him a drink. I'd be the one pushing the other girls out of the way so I could have his attention.

He stared at me for several seconds, his stony expression absorbing my words like it took a few moments to process them. I just gave him the biggest compliment of his life. "Doesn't mean much unless it worked with the right woman."

I held his gaze, the pulse loud in my ears and rampant in my neck. "I still think it would work..."

---

"You drink scotch?" Kent asked in surprise.

"She smokes cigars too." Maverick brought his glass to his lips and took a drink.

I swirled my glass before I brought it to my lips. "My father drank and smoked a lot, so I just picked it up..."

Kent gave me a look of approval before he pivoted his body in the booth and examined the women in the bar. With predatory eyes, he scanned the room for a warm body to take home.

I imagined Maverick did the same thing—but tonight, he wasn't.

His arm was around my shoulders, and his body was pressed close to mine. Sometimes his fingers dug into my hair gently, the touch light and sexy. With his thighs spread apart under the table and his shoulders looking broad in his suit, he was the hottest man in the joint.

And he was my husband.

"What about her?" Kent nodded to the blonde in the corner. "She doesn't look like a weirdo who will ask for my number later."

"Asking for a number makes a woman a weirdo?" I asked.

Kent shrugged. "You meet a woman in a bar to hook up. Pretty self-explanatory."

"But you might want to hook up again. And you'll be glad you have that number."

"I doubt it." Kent looked at me before he turned back to the girls. "What do you think, Maverick?"

He stared at the girls and shrugged. "They all look the same to me. I would just pick one and go for it."

"You know…" Kent turned back to Maverick. "You're a lot more boring as a married man." He finished his drink and left the glass on the table before he scooted out of the booth and buttoned the front of his jacket. Then he walked up to a brunette standing at the edge of the bar and initiated a conversation.

Maverick turned back to me. "Want another?"

"I've had enough for tonight." I pushed my glass away so I couldn't be tempted anymore.

"You don't seem drunk."

"I hold my liquor well—like a lady."

"I think ladies don't drink much in the first place."

"Then I'm not a lady."

He chuckled as he looked at me, the smile reaching the corners of his mouth.

My hand moved to his thigh under the table, and I resisted the urge to press my face into his neck and close my eyes. My body wanted to relax into this man, to be as affectionate as I wanted. It was past midnight, and I'd already had such a long evening… and he looked as comfortable as a pillow. "You can join Kent if you want. You don't have to stay here because of me…"

Maverick looked into my gaze and watched me for a long time, his eyes focused like nothing would interrupt his concentration. His fingers moved in my hair slightly, and his thumb brushed against my cheek. He was a rough man, but he could be so gentle when he wanted to be. He could be anything he wanted to be…if that's what he wanted. "You know this is the only place I want to be."

---

MY EYES WERE LOCKED on to his beautiful brown eyes, and my entire body was on fire. I could come a million more times if he lasted that long, but I'd already enjoyed myself plenty of times to get through the night. My nails clawed at his muscular torso, and I got off on watching his perfect body work to fuck me.

His muscular arms were pinned behind my knees, and his strong back arched to pound into me at an ideal pace, kissing my clit with his hard stomach and then doing it again just a second later. His enormous dick buried itself deep inside me every time, hitting the perfect spot like a finger to a button. He kept tapping it over and over again, making my body convulse in euphoria.

He'd worked long enough to please me, and it was time for him to reap his reward. I grabbed his hips and directed his pace. "Your turn…" I bit my bottom lip as I guided him back and forward, forcing him to slow and down and finish. He thickened slightly inside me, his dick pressing hard against every side of my channel and giving it a final stretch before he released.

His body relaxed before the final shudder, the final bucks of his hips that were accompanied by a sexy moan that filled the bedroom. It was the sexiest noise he'd ever made, a masculine hum that complemented the dark furniture and deep tones of his bedroom. He rested his forehead against mine as he finished filling the tip of the condom, his chest more beautiful when it was covered with a shiny gleam of sweat.

My hands moved to his ass, and I gripped both cheeks just as he did to me.

He smiled slightly before he pulled out of me and walked into the bathroom to dispose of the condom.

I'd considered asking him to stop wearing condoms altogether. I'd been on the pill for a long time, and I didn't see the point in wearing something if we were both clean. But if we wanted to do that, it would mean monogamy. It seemed like Maverick was already in that place, but what if he wasn't? What if I pushed for more and got his rejection instead? I decided to let him make the decision when he was ready.

My eyes felt heavy because it was already after one in the morning. It'd been such a long night, but so deeply magical that I wouldn't change anything. I sang my heart out at the opera, having no idea that my husband was sitting in the audience watching me.

Maverick came to bed, turned off the light, and then got under the covers with me.

I knew he wasn't on speaking terms with his father, but I expected Maverick to figure out what I'd done eventually. He hadn't mentioned it, so I assumed Caspian had kept that information to himself.

What would Maverick think once he found out?

He pressed his hard chest against my back and wrapped his arm around my waist. His face rested against the back of my neck, his nose buried in my hair. The darkness surrounded us both, our bodies warm in the luxurious bed.

I was so tired, but I didn't want to sleep. I wanted to stay there forever, to live in the moment. Wordlessly, we snuggled together, his fingers resting against my left hand where my wedding ring sat on my finger. I'd gotten so used to his bed that I never wanted to sleep in mine alone.

There was never a more comfortable place other than the one right here—next to him.

## 10

# MAVERICK

"You're so pussy-whipped."

I sat at my desk in the office across the hall from my bedroom. With a cigar in my mouth and my laptop in front of me, I worked while Kent talked on speakerphone. "I'm pussy-whipped, but not in the way you're suggesting."

"I disagree. You're so hung up on her."

"I am married to her…"

Kent chuckled. "Man, I remember when you told me you didn't give a damn about her. It would be easier if she got hit by a car and died or something."

Hearing that sentiment repeated back to me made me sick. It was hard to believe I'd said those words—and meant them. But now, I didn't want anything bad to ever happen to her. She wasn't a burden in my life. She was the one thing I looked forward to the most. "Things change."

"Which is why I'm saying you're pussy-whipped."

"I wouldn't take it that far. I've always been obsessed with pussy."

"But you're obsessed with just one, specifically."

"Whatever. My libido is the same." I took a puff and let the smoke float from my mouth. It was midafternoon, a little early for a cigar, but the urge had hit me. "What happened with your lady?"

"We humped, then she left."

I chuckled. "That's a nice way to put it."

"Paints a vivid picture, huh?" His laugh echoed back at me. "So, are your bachelor days over? If so, I need to find a new wingman."

Technically, I was married. My bachelor days ended a long time ago. "I don't know... I wouldn't put it like that."

"You seem committed to her. It would be stupid to argue."

"I am committed to her. She's my wife, and it's my job to take care of her. But I wouldn't say I'm committed to her sexually. We'll have our fun, but it'll eventually burn out like all other relationships. We'll go back to sleeping with other people. Then we'll do it all over again..."

"That's romantic," he said sarcastically.

"A lot of men have mistresses. Keeps the relationship healthy. There's no man on earth who can honestly say he's happy with monogamy that spans decades. It's not natural. It makes everything stale."

"If that's how you really feel, you might want to tell her that."

"She knows." We'd talked about it in the past, about casual sex between husband and wife. She would have her lovers, and I would have mine.

"I don't think she does, man. I see the way she looks at you..."

I was tired of talking about my love life. "I'll swing by later today for the game. Talk to you then."

"Fine, blow me off." He hung up.

I hit the button on the speaker and kept working, the cigar still sitting in my mouth.

A few minutes later, Arwen poked her head into the room. "Working in here today?"

"Just paperwork." I set the cigar on the rim of the ashtray.

She strode into the room while swaying her hips, looking sexy in a sweater dress with black leggings underneath. She had the kind of body that could pull off any kind of outfit. Right now, she looked like a perfect ten.

I kept staring at her instead of my computer.

She grabbed the cigar and smashed it into the glass bowl. "You smoke too much."

"Occasionally."

"If you smoke too much occasionally, you still smoke too much."

I grinned slightly at her wit.

"I'm serious. Cancer is a real thing."

"I'm not scared of cancer."

Her face suddenly turned cold.

I didn't realize what I'd said until the idiotic words were already out of my mouth. They were insensitive and stupid. "I didn't mean it like that… I'm sorry." Her father passed away from lung cancer, and he wasn't a heavy smoker. There was no reason why the same thing wouldn't happen to me.

She dropped her glare. "I don't want you smoking anymore."

"I don't see the harm in lighting up once in a while."

"Once in a while is like twice a year. Every week is not once in a while. You're technically a smoker."

I shrugged. "It suits me."

"Well, it doesn't suit me." She came around my desk and opened the top drawer where my stash was. She grabbed them and stuffed them into her pocket so she could throw them away later.

"I don't appreciate you telling me what to do."

"Join the club." She returned to the front of the desk, copping an attitude no one else could pull off. "I want you to live a long time, Maverick. And not just to keep me safe." She turned around and walked out, her perfect ass shaking back and forth.

I stared at it until she was out the door.

Now, my dick was hard in my jeans, and I couldn't remember what I was working on.

Only one thing was on my mind.

SHE WAS SUPPOSED to leave for work at the opera, but I had other things on my mind.

I had her on all fours on my bed, her back beautifully arched and her perky ass pointed to the sky. My hand dug into my nightstand, bumping against the wedding ring I hadn't worn since my wedding day, until I found a condom to roll down my dick.

"I'm gonna be so late..." She looked at me over her shoulder, her pussy gleaming as the slickness dripped from her entrance.

"Doesn't look like you care." I got onto the bed, my knees sinking into the mattress on either side of her hips. I pointed my head at the open slit and slowly pushed inside, getting through the first squeeze until my shaft glided inside. My hands gripped her waist, and I slowly inched deeper and deeper, pushing through her slick tightness until my entire base was sheathed.

She moaned when she felt all of me, her hands gripping the sheets underneath her.

Nothing made me feel more alive than this—being buried inside a woman. With her beautiful ass in my face, her little asshole on display, and such a sexy back, she was perfect. Her brown curtain of hair stretched down her shoulder blades, perfectly styled for the performance she was about to give.

But I was going to fuck her before that happened.

I held on to her hips and tugged her into me as I thrust,

giving it to her deep the entire time. I was in the mood to sink deep inside of her pussy, to have every inch covered to the hilt. I wanted to feel her intimately, claim her before an auditorium of men gawked at her.

She was gorgeous—and she was mine.

I grabbed a fistful of hair and gave a gentle tug. "You want to go?" She was bouncing her ass back at me, her back arching deeper to get the angle just perfect. She moaned continuously, each separate cry fusing together into one long tremble. "Sheep, I asked you a question."

She clawed at the sheets harder. "No..."

"You want your husband to keep fucking you?"

She bounced back on my dick a little harder. "Yes..."

I stared at the beautiful woman underneath me as I continued to fuck her, continued to get the greatest pleasure around my dick. It was so good, feeling her slickness like that. It was the best pussy I'd ever fucked, best pussy I'd ever looked at. "Good. This is going to be a while."

## 11

## ARWEN

My thoughts drifted back to my husband often.

Every minute of the day.

When we weren't together, I wondered what he was doing. When he was inside me, I wondered if he enjoyed me as much as I enjoyed him. He was the best sex I'd ever had, the best man I'd ever been with. The idea of going to someone else when I had him at home every night seemed absurd.

Marrying him started off as a nightmare...but somehow turned into a fairy tale.

I barely made it in time before the show started. But I certainly had no regrets. I was thoroughly pleased before I had to stand in heels for two hours and sing loud enough to shatter glass.

I stepped onto the stage, gave my performance, and like every other night, it went quickly. Time passed differently during a performance. There was so much to do and focus on, there was barely any time to think about anything else.

When the show ended, I returned backstage and sat at my vanity. Now I always hoped Maverick would appear behind me, giving me a kiss after my performance. I pulled the pins out of my hair then ran my fingers through the strands. My false eyelashes and lipstick were removed next. When I sensed a heated stare on my face, my heart started to race. I could feel his intensity. My lips softened into a smile because I knew I would see his espresso eyes when I looked in the reflection.

When I lifted my gaze to look, I saw someone else.

A pair of blue eyes stared back at me from a square face. A hard jawline led to a square jaw, every single square tooth visible in his strange smile. Maybe it was a smile to him, but it looked like a grimace to everyone else. His other features were difficult to determine in the small mirror, but he seemed to be tall—abnormally tall.

When my eyes focused more, he stepped out of the line of the mirror and disappeared.

---

WITH MY CLUTCH IN HAND, I left out the back door and took the steps to the sidewalk. My car was parked a few yards away, the only car in the parking lot because I was one of the last people to leave.

My heels echoed against the concrete once I reached the sidewalk. I hadn't brought my coat, so I had to suffer the cold evening air on just my bare skin. My dress was thin, but backstage was so stuffy that anything thicker would be a million degrees too hot.

## The Wolf and His Wife 143

Soon, I wasn't the only set of footsteps in the area.

Another set accompanied mine—distinct and heavy.

I didn't turn around to make it obvious, but the approach unnerved me. There was no other car in the parking lot, so where was this person going? And judging from the heaviness of the thuds, it was definitely a man.

Then I noticed two men emerged from separate directions.

I started to panic.

I pulled my phone out of my clutch, doing my best to seem casual even though I was fucking terrified. Three men were converging on me, and now it was overwhelmingly obvious what their intention was.

I wished Maverick were there.

But he was twenty minutes away.

I kept walking, unsure what to do. If I sprinted into a run, one of them would catch me in seconds. There was nowhere for me to go. Nowhere for me to hide. I took my one shot and pulled up Maverick's name on the phone.

The second I hit send, the guy behind me took off.

"Ah!" In heels, I ran as fast as I could and dropped my clutch in the process. My phone was still in my hand, and I dodged into the passageway between the theater and the bank beside me. All I could hear was the fear in my deep breathing, the terror I felt as my heart worked to pump enough blood into my system. "Shit, help! Help!" I called for anyone to help me, hoped Maverick was listening over the line. With a quick look on his GPS, he could figure out where I was.

"Shut your mouth." An enormous hand grabbed the back of my head and slammed me into the wall. "No one is gonna help you."

My body collided with the wall, and the air left my lungs. I barely had time to stuff my phone down the front of my dress and slip it in my bra. "Let go of me!" I kicked back.

This man was bigger than a horse, so it was like kicking a mountain. He laughed then pressed me into the wall until I was squished like a bug. "I was gonna take you home, but after seeing how pretty you are when you sing...I think I'll fuck you now." He yanked up my dress and pushed down my panties.

This couldn't be happening. "Let me go."

"Fight, bitch. I was hoping you would." He pushed me against the wall again and grabbed both of my wrists with a single hand. He was more than a foot taller than me, a fucking giant. He pressed my cheek hard against the wall then forced his big dick right between my ass cheeks. "Damn, you have a nice ass."

I wanted to scream for Maverick, but I couldn't say a word. My eyes watered in panic, and I wanted to give up because there was nothing else I could do. This was the beginning of the end, the start of a life of torture that would kill me. "Please..."

"Please beg." He spoke in my ear. "It's one of my kinks."

I tried to buck him off, but it was no use. I would just break my back in the process.

His dick throbbed against my ass cheeks, a monster with its own brain. "You have a small cunt, so it'll be a tight fit. But we'll make it work." He licked his palm and smeared it along his crown and base.

A police car drove past the street, the lights and sirens on. They weren't coming for me, but they were enough of a distraction to make my assailant turn to look.

Then I dropped down and hit the ground.

He grabbed me by the hair and tried to yank me back. "There's no running from this, baby."

My teeth clenched down on his hand, and I bit him like a damn animal. Blood gushed into my mouth and everywhere else.

The man yanked his hand back, but he chuckled like it was a game. "You want to play rough, huh?"

I got to my feet and sprinted. I ran across the street, almost got hit by a car, and kept running. There were only a few cars on the road but no pedestrians. The ones who were around immediately cowered away when they saw the commotion.

I fished the phone out of my dress. "Maverick!"

"I'm coming to get you!" He spoke a million miles an hour, knowing I didn't have time. "You're on del Corso?"

"Yes."

"Turn left."

I would have asked why under normal circumstances, but this wasn't normal. I ran as hard as I could, ignoring the aches from my feet and the possibility of breaking my ankle in my heels. Years in show business taught me how to move in the damn things. "I'm going."

"Keep going past the next two stop signs."

"I can't run that long!"

"You're gonna have to!"

I didn't look back as I kept running, crossing traffic just to confuse the asshole behind me.

"There's a narrow alleyway with a blue bicycle to your left. Take it."

I did it without hesitation.

"Keep going until you see another narrow passageway with clothes on a line."

I turned left, getting into a tighter space between two buildings.

"Left."

I was going back in the direction I came, back to the busy street.

"Cross the street and go left."

"I can't keep this up for long—"

"Do what I say." The sound of his revving engine was in the background.

I kept going.

He directed me through various passageways, getting me away from the assholes without covering much ground. I kept going, crossing streets and turning in circles as I shook off my attackers.

I'd passed the same building a couple of times. When I rounded it for the third time, he told me to go inside.

"What? I can't get in there."

"There's a keypad on the entrance. Find it."

There were double glass doors leading to some kind of private entrance. I found the keypad on the left. "Got it."

"Type in 64831 then pound."

My breathing was haywire, and I could barely keep my fingers straight. I somehow didn't make any mistakes, even though I was losing my shit.

"You should have enough time before they catch up with you."

A beep sounded and the doors opened.

"Get inside."

I stepped inside the doors, and they closed a second later.

"Take the elevator to the third floor."

I got inside and hit the button. I leaned against the wall and tried to catch my breath, my feet bloody and my dress torn. The door opened to a loft.

"Disable the elevator by hitting the blue button."

I didn't care if I could never get to the bottom floor. I smashed that button with my palm so damn hard, I nearly broke my hand. The doors opened, and I stepped into a living room, decorated in the same style as Maverick's home. "What is this place?"

"It's my place in the city. There's a pistol hidden underneath the coffee table."

I got on my hands and knees and grabbed it. It was the first time I'd ever held a gun, and now I realized just how heavy it was. It must be loaded with this amount of weight. Feeling it in my hand reminded me this nightmare wasn't over. That giant could crawl up the side of the building like an animal if he really wanted to.

"I have to go, Arwen."

"Wait, hold on." He couldn't help me over the phone, but letting his voice guide me was an immense comfort. "What's gonna happen?"

"I'm almost to the city. My men have been dispatched, so we'll scare him away from the area. Keep your eyes trained on the door. I'll be there as soon as I can."

"How are you going to get up here?"

"The stairs."

"Oh…of course, there are stairs."

"Keep that gun, but I'm sure you won't have to use it."

I leaned against the wall and slid to the floor, terrified because that cruel man could still get to me. He'd lifted up my dress and pushed his hard dick against my ass like he owned me. I'd never felt so violated, so disgusted. If he walked through that door, I would empty that clip so fucking fast.

"I'm gonna be the one that walks through that door, alright? Don't shoot."

"Okay..."

"I'll be there as soon as I can."

I wanted him there now. I wanted my wolf. "Please hurry..." I kept the tears out of my voice but barely. I'd never needed this man more in my life than I did right then. If it weren't for him, no one else would help me. I would be snatched off the street and raped and tortured. He was the only person who actually gave a damn about me. "Please..."

---

TWENTY MINUTES LATER, a door opened.

I rose to my feet and pointed the gun, my finger on the trigger even though I didn't know how to use it. I just needed to look formidable, at the least.

But thankfully, it was Maverick.

Dressed in a black t-shirt and jeans, his muscled frame entered the apartment, and his concerned expression landed on me.

I set the gun on the counter, relieved I didn't have to use it. My shoes were on the carpet, coated in blood from my feet. My dress was ripped in the places where that asshole had grabbed me. But now that my gaze took in Maverick, I knew I would be safe.

With pain-filled eyes, he walked toward me, his expression anxious.

I threw myself into his arms and rested my face against his chest, relaxing for the first time since the chase started. Shedding tears in front of other people was something I never did, but with him, I showed my most vulnerable side without caring. Tears soaked into his t-shirt, and I gripped him around the waist as I shook in his embrace.

His hand cupped the back of my head, and he rested his lips against my forehead. "Sheep, it's okay…"

"Did you kill him?" When that man was dead, it really would be okay.

His silence gave me the answer I didn't want to hear.

I pulled away and looked into his expression, not caring that I looked like absolute hell.

His hand moved to my cheek, his thumb grazing over my soft skin. His eyes shifted back and forth slightly as he looked into mine, like he was absorbing all my pain into himself. "By the time I got here, he and his men had scattered."

"Kill him, Maverick. I want you to kill him." I was ordering someone's death like an executioner, but I didn't feel any remorse for it. If I hadn't been able to slip away, he would have raped me right in that alleyway, then did it again…and again.

His hands moved to my arms, and he gave me a gentle squeeze. "I will."

I got what I wanted, but I still wasn't satisfied. "He yanked up my dress and almost raped me—"

"Please." It was the first time he dropped his gaze, like he couldn't handle the horror story I was about to tell. "Just don't..." He stared at the ground for a couple of seconds before he lifted his gaze to meet mine.

When I saw the hurt on his face, I knew how real this was. I knew this wasn't just a relationship we were forced to be in. We really were husband and wife. We really were a team that would do anything for each other.

"I'll kill him," he whispered. "I promise."

"Do you know him?"

"He was the one who showed up at my gates that night. He was one of the men your father crossed."

Now I was livid with my father for being so stupid. "Why did my father have to get involved in that?"

"I know what he did was wrong, but I'm sure he had no idea what it would turn into. Your father was a good man who loved you, who would do anything for you. Don't hate him."

It was the last thing I'd expected Maverick to say. "Thank you for coming... Thank you for protecting me... I don't know what to say. I can't even begin to express how grateful I am that I have you." More tears poured from my eyes, but now they weren't from fear. My affection for this man had deepened to a whole new level. I respected him, admired him...and would die for him.

He circled his arms around me and pulled me into his chest. His hand rested against the back of my neck while he cradled me, letting me shed my tears onto his clothes and skin. "I'll always be your wolf, Sheep."

## 12

## MAVERICK

I HID MY ANGER FROM HER.

The last thing she needed was to see me blow up and lose my mind.

I was livid that Kamikaze pulled this stunt right under my nose. He basically declared war on the DeVille family.

Good thing my wife was smart enough to get away.

I was sure that pissed him off.

I drove back into the countryside with her in the passenger seat. Her dress was ripped in the places where he'd grabbed her, and her feet were bloody from running for her life. With her cheek tilted toward the window, she watched the darkness blur past outside. She hadn't said more than two words since we got into the car.

My knuckles were white because I gripped the steering wheel so hard. I was livid that someone had tried to attack her on her way to her car, but I was also pissed that

Kamikaze had crossed me like that. I refused to sell her, so he decided just to take her.

Now we openly despised each other.

It would result in a war with lots of causalities…like I didn't have enough on my plate already.

But that wasn't her fault. She couldn't control her beauty, the fascinating allure that surrounded her. And whenever she opened her mouth to sing…she captured the hearts of everyone in the room. Kamikaze fell under her spell just the way I had so many times…so he had to steal her from me.

Killing Kamikaze wouldn't be easy. He had a lot of loyal men, men who wouldn't stop fighting until their skulls were demolished by bullets. This wasn't the last attempt he would make. He would try again.

So I had to kill him.

It would be much easier if I weren't at war with my father right now. He had a horde of men I could use. Not to mention, he had a disturbed mind obsessed with bloodlust, so he was the perfect ally to have at the moment.

But Arwen had fucked that up.

We returned to the house and walked inside, most of the lights off because it was past midnight. I didn't ask if she wanted something to eat because she probably didn't have an appetite.

We headed to the stairs and started to walk up.

She winced, grabbing the banister for support. Her eyes closed, and she grimaced like the pain in her feet was simply too much.

She was lighter than air, so it was easy for me to scoop her into my arms and pull her to my chest. One arm supported her shoulders while the other hooked underneath her knees. With her cheek pressed into my shirt, I carried her the rest of the way.

I stepped into my bedroom and set her on the bed, feeling the defeat in her limbs. She lay down right away, like she had no energy to remove her torn dress from her body. Kamikaze disturbed her so much that she was practically broken.

With lifeless eyes, she lay there, probably remembering the horrific event again and again.

I pulled the zipper down on the back and got the ruined dress loose before I removed it altogether. I tossed it into the hamper with the intention of throwing it out in the morning. She wouldn't want a reminder of what happened tonight.

I took off her panties too, knowing she wouldn't want those either.

I pulled the sheets down and tucked her inside before I removed my clothes and set my gun on the nightstand. I went into the bathroom and did my nightly routine, washing my face and brushing my teeth before I returned.

She hadn't moved.

I turned off the lamp before I got into bed beside her, her back facing me.

I'd already saved her, but that wasn't enough. She'd had a taste of my world, the cruel reality of dealing with men like me. She'd saved those women from the barn, but she'd never imagined she would be in their shoes herself.

I pressed my chest to her back and wrapped my arm around her waist, reminding her I was there. Surrounded by these four walls and an indestructible fortress, no one could touch us. And even if they could, I would be the last man standing. "You're safe, Sheep. I won't let anything happen to you…I promise." I'd made a vow to her father that I would protect her from the psychopaths that wanted to use her, but my commitment didn't stem from just that. I wanted to keep her safe because that's what she deserved…not to be assaulted in an alleyway.

She turned around and faced me, her blue eyes gazing into mine like she thought I was her hero. Her fingers gently touched my arm, and she was nude under the sheets, her tits barely covered by the thin fabric. She was naked and beautiful, but sex wasn't on my mind. "I know you will, Maverick. It all happened so fast… I haven't had time to process it until now. I was in survival mode and just trying to get to the next place. But now that I'm here, safe and sound, I'm more disgusted by that man than I was before."

He was garbage. "I'll kill him. He won't be around for long."

"He's enormous…the guy was like seven feet tall."

"Doesn't matter how big he is. He bleeds like everyone else." A bullet to the skull would kill him just like it would kill me. In hand-to-hand combat, it might be a little different. If he landed a single punch in the wrong spot, he could kill me. But I had speed to compensate for that.

"I still don't want anything to happen to you. I want him dead, but I don't want to lose you in the process." She had been terrified just minutes ago, but now she was worried about me. When her mascara was smeared down her face and her lips were tight with unease, she somehow looked more alluring. When she was scared, she allowed me to console her...and that was sexy.

"No matter what, he needs to die. He crossed me, and I can't let that go unpunished. And if I don't kill him, he'll just try to take you again. In his eyes, you're already his property. You're his investment."

"I'm no one's property—except yours."

I did my best to control my dick's reaction, but it was in vain. My cock hardened automatically at her confession, growing plump and full of blood. But I kept my mind in the game, focusing on what mattered. "He was at the party where you played the piano. We spoke privately while you sang, and he offered me more money. When I refused, he offered me a cut of your profits."

Her cheeks drained of blood and turned pale. Shock entered her gaze, like her mind couldn't believe something so vile.

"Then it became clear that he was planning to get you one way or another—so I might as well take his money."

"Who the hell does he think he is? My father may have scammed him, but that's not my problem."

"That's not how the real world works, unfortunately."

Her eyes filled with rage, offended that she could be seen as a product rather than a person.

"I have to kill him before he kills me. No other way around it."

"Can I help?"

I wouldn't let her be anywhere near him again. "No. I have to take care of this on my own."

"How? You've got men and he's got men. This will be a war."

"Unless I can figure out a better way of doing it..." An idea came to mind, but I wasn't thrilled about it. It only left me a fifty percent chance of survival, and those odds simply weren't good enough for me. "They call him Kamikaze for a reason. He's unhinged and a psychopath He's just as likely to kill himself as he is to kill his enemies. He's unafraid of death, so he does crazy-ass shit. That gives him the upper hand because you never know what he might do next."

"I hate this guy more and more..."

"Sometimes, when he's at a stalemate, he plays Russian roulette with his enemies."

When her eyes widened, it was obvious she knew exactly what that entailed.

"He's pulled the trigger on himself before...but he managed to survive." A bullet shattered his skull and sank into his brain, but doctors were somehow able to remove it and keep him breathing. He didn't lose any mental abilities.

"And he still plays it?" she asked incredulously. "That didn't deter him?"

"No. That's why they call him Kamikaze."

"Well, you aren't doing that. We'll find another way..." She scooted closer to me and rested her head against my chest.

I didn't want my life to be decided by a lone bullet in a barrel, but Kamikaze was too powerful of an opponent to conquer on my own—without my father's help. I was just as likely to die in bullet warfare as I was to roll the dice.

How could my life be worth gambling for Arwen'? She was someone I'd been forced to marry, someone I didn't even want when we first met. But now, I really did see myself as her husband...and that's what husbands should do. They should do whatever it took to protect their wife...even if it meant their own death in the process.

---

I WOKE up the next morning with her on top of me. She was snuggled so close, her body using mine as a crutch to get through the night. She seemed to feel safer the closer she was. When we were practically a single person, she felt the most secure.

After what she'd been through, I let her get away with whatever she wanted.

My hand stroked her hair, and I admired her beautiful face, loving the beautiful fairness of her cheeks. There wasn't even a freckle on her skin, making her look like a porcelain doll. She had the face that could grace billboards and star in commercials. But instead of being a famous face, she was in my bed.

I stared at her for another minute before I rolled her to her back then scooted out from between the sheets. I skipped a shower and pulled on my clothes before I quietly slipped out the door. I headed downstairs, skipped breakfast, and went to my office at the factory. My workers were producing twice the amount of product we normally shipped, but since my cheese was in demand, we had a lot of orders to fill.

I took advantage of the privacy in my office and made the call I'd been thinking about all night. If I were to avoid it altogether, it would make me seem like a pussy. I didn't have a plan right that second, but it was better to face him without a clue than avoid him instead. I made the call and held the phone to my ear.

Ring.

Ring.

Maybe that asshole wouldn't pick up.

Ring.

His booming voice came over the line, like we were old friends sharing an inside joke. "Maverick. I thought I would be hearing from you today. Was hoping to see you in person...but this will do."

"Trust me, you don't want to see me in person right now."

He laughed. "Ooh...big man."

I was glad my father and I got out of the business when we did. I didn't have the energy to deal with crazy people anymore. Kamikaze was a pain in the ass, and every second he was still alive was obnoxious. "I warned you not to cross me."

"I know," he said with a chuckle. "But all of that went out the window when you lied. I have a debt that needs to be repaid, and your little bitch owes me."

"Lied about what?" I never told him a lie because we hardly spoke to each other. I spent most of my time not talking rather than digging myself into a hole I couldn't get out of. "I have better things to do than be a coward."

Instead of laughing, he turned quiet and formidable. "Maverick, I know your marriage is a hoax. You cut a deal to get what you needed—and I respect that. But you need to respect the fact that her father owes me millions—and she's going to give it to me. We can still be allies. This doesn't need to get ugly. We just need to understand each other."

I looked out the window, but I couldn't enjoy the beautiful fall morning we were having. There was dew on the grass and the leaves of the trees. The summer heat had faded away, replaced by an inviting breeze that licked the sweat off the skin. But all I could feel was the deep pounding of my heart, the shock that his announcement gave me. My marriage was bogus, but I didn't expect him to know that. He seemed confident in his assessment, so someone must have told him...but only a couple people knew the truth.

"Just give her to me, Maverick. You can go back to your bachelor life, and I can get what's mine. We both walk away winners."

My dreams would be haunted by her face, and my heart would be scarred by the guilt. I wouldn't be able to close my eyes without thinking about what was happening to her, whether it was Kamikaze or some sheik who'd traveled across the ocean to pay a fortune to fuck her. I'd rather blow my brains out then carry that burden. "Despite what you've heard, it's not a hoax…at least, not anymore. She's my wife and she's mine. She's not for sale, and she's not for the taking."

He was dead quiet, like the phone might have lost the signal. "Looks like her value just went up."

My heart dropped into my stomach.

"She steals the obsession of every man around her… including Maverick DeVille. Her pussy must be one hell of a ride."

"Don't talk about my wife like that."

The sick bastard laughed. "It's nothing personal, Maverick. She's the best investment I'm going to find, and I won't stop until I get her. I suggest you save your own ass and let it be. If you force me to kill you, I will."

Now the line had been drawn in the sand, and there was no going back. War had been declared. My only two options were to fight or surrender.

And I definitely wouldn't surrender. "It looks like you're forcing me to kill you. And I will."

---

I SHOT two of his men near the front gates and barged into the house from the rear. I knew my childhood home better than he realized, and sneaking into the place wasn't difficult. I broke the window instead of picking the lock just to be an ass.

I made my way inside and found him sitting in the dining room.

*The Wolf and His Wife* 163

Instead of pulling out my gun and pointing it at his head, I stilled in the entryway and stared at him.

He was alone. A decanter of scotch sat beside him along with a full glass in his fingertips. The remains of his dinner looked like fish with a side of lemon. On the wall was a painting of my mother on their wedding day. There was no way for him to have known I was coming, not when I killed his men and got here so quickly.

So this was really him.

Sitting alone in the dark—booze for company.

He looked up and met my gaze, not the least bit surprised by my appearance.

That meant my suspicion was right—he betrayed me.

I stepped into the room, my pistol sitting on my hip. My footsteps sounded loud against the hardwood floor, just the way my mother's heels used to echo when she carried dinner into the room.

He kept his hand on his glass like it was a life raft.

I stopped in front of him, stared into those heartless eyes, and then drew my weapon.

He still didn't flinch. He looked at me and ignored the barrel pointed right in his face. "Perfect solution. Kamikaze wants to torture her—and I want that woman to be tortured." He brought the glass to his lips and took a long drink.

I cocked the gun. "And you're willing to die for that solution?"

"Die?" he asked. "You're my son. I know how weak you are."

I pressed the tip of the barrel right against his skull.

He still didn't react. "Then do it."

My hand started to shake as my finger held the trigger. All I had to do was make a quick squeeze and his brains would explode on the wall behind him. My mother was dead, and my father would join her. It was probably exactly what he wanted—since there was nothing left for him in the land of the living.

With a bored expression on his face, he watched the gun shake in my hand. "You aren't going to do it, so don't bother with the gesture." He lifted his hand and gently pushed my gun aside.

I dropped it, feeling like less of a man for not pulling the trigger. "That's the difference between you and me. You're an asshole who will kill his own son. I won't kill my own father."

"It's still better than threatening to do something that you'll never do. It hurts your credibility, makes you seem weak. Next time you point that gun at my head, have some balls and actually shoot. At least I'll have some respect for you if you do."

My shoulders sagged in defeat, and I stared at my father with new eyes. Just when I thought my opinion couldn't get any lower, he somehow made it possible. "I can't kill you because you're going to help me."

"Do what?" he asked, his eyebrow raised.

"You started this mess with Kamikaze. You'll finish it."

His eyes shifted away, and he chuckled. "Actually, I didn't..."

His underlying meaning hung in the air, but he never elaborated. He kept whatever secret he had to himself.

I refused to play his game, so I didn't ask. "We're going to take him out together. I'm not letting him take my wife."

"Stop calling her that. She's just a pawn in a big chess game."

"No. You're the pawn now." I tapped his shoulder with my gun. "You're going to help me keep her safe."

"I'm not, Maverick. I wouldn't have told Kamikaze the truth if that were the case. He'll get rid of her, and that will fix our problems."

"No, it'll fix your problem…if you can even call it a problem. Mom is dead. Arwen isn't going to change that."

"But she's a little bitch who deserves what's coming to her." He clenched his jaw as if he hated her more than Ramon.

Now I looked at my father with new eyes. He was a psychopath like Kamikaze, just in his own way. "You did a really fucked-up thing when you went behind my back and told Kamikaze the marriage is bogus. If you ever want to make it up to me, you'll help me kill him. Otherwise, I'll never forgive you."

He took another drink of his scotch, uninterested in what I'd said. "All I care about is putting that little bitch in the ground. I don't care about your forgiveness, and I certainly don't want it."

Why couldn't I just lift my gun and kill him on the spot? Was my father right when he called me weak? He was just as guilty as Kamikaze. He didn't deserve a free pass just because of our relationship. He wouldn't hesitate to kill me, so I should do the same. But when I looked at that man, I still saw childhood memories. I still saw birthday parties and afternoons when he taught me how to kick a ball. I still remembered Christmas and every other beautiful moment we had.

So I couldn't do it.

I was livid that he'd risked my wife.

I was livid that he was a terrible father.

I was livid that he became such a piece of shit.

But I still couldn't do it.

Maybe I was weak.

I turned around and left the dining room, unable to stare at his arrogant expression a moment longer. I turned around at the threshold and barely made eye contact when I said my final words. "If Mother is watching down on us right now... she's so disappointed in you."

---

"I HAVE A SHOW TONIGHT, but I don't know what to do. After what happened the other night...I'm not sure I want to go back." She stared at her dress with her back turned to me, her arms crossed over her chest. Her perfect frame was beautiful in just the black thong she wore, her curves so enticing, I was practically salivating.

I wanted to throw her onto the bed and fuck her.

But it would be insensitive to rush into things. I'd heard her whimpers and cries over the phone when Kamikaze had her pinned. I heard him threaten to rape her right in the open. I didn't have a visual on the moment, but the mental picture was enough to haunt me. She was the one who actually lived it. "I'll send my men with you. They'll keep you safe."

"No." She eyed a black dress hanging in front of her, but she didn't take it. "I don't trust anyone."

"You can't give up your part in the opera. Don't let some asshole make you change your life."

"It's a small compromise not to be raped." She shut the closet doors and turned back to me, her perfect tits on display.

It was hard to have a serious conversation with her when she looked like that. I kept my eyes locked on to hers and resisted the temptation to stare at her hard nipples and beautiful curves. "I'll go with you."

She tightened her arms across her chest, blocking her tits from view. "You will?"

I nodded. "I'll sit in the audience. And then I'll walk you to your car." I wasn't much better than a group of men assigned to the job, but she obviously felt more comfortable with me than anyone else. I had other things to do, like plotting my revenge against Kamikaze, but I couldn't let Arwen give up all her joys because of her fear.

"You'd do that?"

"You must know by now that I would do anything for you." When I drove to Florence to rescue her from Kamikaze, I was putting my life on the line. Anytime I went head-to-head with that man, it was a dangerous game. He didn't play by the rules like everyone else, so you never knew what trick he might pull. He didn't exactly have a code of ethics like most people. That was probably why he'd survived so many decades.

Arwen's father's cancer was a bit of unexpected luck, if you asked me. He'd died on a morphine drip in the hospital, holding his daughter's hand as he passed peacefully in his sleep. If Kamikaze had gotten his hands on him, his death would have been excruciating.

"I just know you're busy..."

"This isn't forever." I opened the doors of her closet and grabbed the black dress off the hanger. "I'll take care of him eventually, and you'll have your freedom back. You'll have more freedom than you've ever had before."

"When are you going to kill him?" She unzipped the back of the dress and began to step into it.

"Not sure yet." How did you kill a monster like that without losing too many men in the process? If nuclear weapons weren't so destructive, that would be a good option. "But let me worry about that."

She got the dress on then turned around so I could zip it up the rest of the way.

I dragged the zipper to the base of her neck, making the dress mold to her perfectly. She had the most fascinating curves, a petite woman who had a real ass and impressive tits. Everything about her was perfect. I hadn't noticed when we first met because I was oblivious to everything around me. I'd decided to hate her before I even met her because of the situation. Maybe if I'd met her in a bar or somewhere else, I would have appreciated her beauty the way everyone else did.

She turned back around, giving me a slight smile even though her eyes were still full of hesitation.

"I confronted my father last night. He's the one who told Kamikaze our marriage was a lie."

Her eyes fell as her lips pressed tightly together.

"That was why Kamikaze went after you. He knows about the deal we made. He considers you to be his, the debt your father never repaid. It's clear that one of us will have to kill each other before we find peace."

"It'd better be you," she whispered. "It has to be you…"

"I know." I wished it were that easy.

She moved into me and pressed her forehead against my chest. Her arms rested on mine, and she closed her eyes, doing her best to stay calm even though it was obvious she was scared. "Let me help you. We can do this together."

"I don't want you anywhere near him."

"But I can be bait. I can lure him out somewhere and—"

"No. I'll take care of it on my own."

She pulled away and lifted her gaze again. "You don't have to. I know you made a promise to my father—"

"That's not the only reason why. You saved those women because it was the right thing to do. I'm going to save you because it's the right thing to do. I would never be able to sleep ever again if something happened to you. So, I will handle this." I wasn't looking forward to the confrontation.

Anytime two armies met on the battlefield, almost all the men died. Bullets were wasted over money, even though both sides were rich. Or they were wasted over women. In some ways, that was worse. I dropped her embrace and pulled away. "We should get going."

## 13

## ARWEN

Knowing Maverick was out there gave me the greatest sense of security I would ever find. He was just one man with one gun, but he made me feel so safe. I preferred his protection over a dozen men who were strangers. At least my husband actually cared about me. He wasn't holding a gun for a paycheck. He was doing it because my life was invaluable to him.

I finished the performance then returned backstage. The cast and crew moved around like every other night, giving each other hugs and kisses in celebration. My eyes kept drifting to the mirror to see the reflection behind me, to make sure the large man with the frightening smile wasn't staring at me like last night. The second we'd made eye contact, a warning burned in my stomach. If I had better sense, I wouldn't have walked to my car by myself in the middle of the night.

I kept looking in the reflection but saw no sign of him. It seemed too obvious to hit me at the opera again, but maybe it was so obvious that it would cause me to drop my guard... making it the perfect opportunity.

I unclasped my earrings then pulled the dozens of pins out of my hair, knowing Maverick would be there any minute.

I'd been struggling with an internal demon for the last few days. All of this happened after I confronted Caspian at the rehab center. Our conversation had to be the trigger that set him off, that made him run to Kamikaze in the first place. That was his punishment for the stunt I pulled.

Seemed harsh to me.

I didn't want to tell Maverick the truth because it would probably piss him off. He would be livid with me for going behind his back once again. But it seemed wrong to leave him in the dark, to not tell him this vital piece of information. If Caspian told Kamikaze that, what else did he say?

Maybe they were both plotting against us.

Maverick appeared behind me, his hands moving to my shoulders as I sat on my stool.

The second I felt his touch, all the tension left the muscles across my frame. An invisible blanket of protection surrounded me, made me feel invincible. His affection was like a drug to me. He made me feel so many degrees of happy.

I pulled the last pin out of my hair and rose to my feet to greet him. Handsome as always, he wore a well-fitted suit with a dark tie. At over six feet, he was tall, dark, and sexy. When I looked into those brown eyes, I knew I never wanted to look at anyone else again. I didn't want to take another lover. I didn't want to meet a man at a bar when I could go home to the man I actually wanted.

And I didn't just want him because of the way he protected me.

His arms slid around my waist. "You were amazing…as always."

"You'd say that even if I weren't."

"True." He smiled as he leaned in and kissed me on the mouth. "But that's a good thing…because you can never go wrong." He kissed me again before he pulled away, stopping the affection before it escalated from PG-13 to X.

"Is this your husband?" Ruby was one of my costars. We sang a duet together in the middle of the show. With pearls around her neck and a smile on her face, she looked Maverick up and down with approval.

"Yes, it is. Maverick this is my costar Ruby."

Maverick took her hand and kissed her on the cheek. "Lovely to meet you."

"You too. Well, I'll let you lovebirds enjoy your night." She walked away behind Maverick then mouthed, "Damn, he's hooooot." She winked then kept walking.

I stopped the smile from spreading across my face.

Maverick had a glint of humor in his eyes, like he knew something.

"What?"

"I'm hot, huh?"

"What are you talking about?" I asked, keeping a straight face.

"There are mirrors everywhere. Tell her I said thank you."

---

Maverick kept his arm around my waist as he walked me to the car. It was dark, with the occasional streetlight illuminating the stairs and sidewalk.

I kept looking up and down the street, waiting to see if three large men would emerge from the shadows.

But no one ever did.

"I have men watching the entire block." He kept his eyes forward as he guided me to the black car. He opened the passenger door. "They aren't here."

I got into the seat, and then we drove away. My eyes kept scanning the darkness for anything unusual until the buildings passed and it was just the open road.

Maverick drove with one hand on the wheel. "He won't try the same thing twice."

"What makes you so sure?"

"Because it would be stupid to repeat the same experiment twice and expect different results. You're on your guard now. I'm armed. It would just be a waste of ammo at this point. He doesn't want to hurt you. He wants you to be in perfect condition for his purpose. So, he's not gonna shoot up the entire street and hope he kills me and all my men without touching you. Too much of a gamble."

*The Wolf and His Wife*

"Do you think he'd try to break in to the house?"

"No. That would require a lot of manpower. The smart thing would be to draw us out somewhere and then do it."

"Well, that's not going to work on me. I'm not going shopping or to the movies anytime soon."

He sped through the darkness while keeping his eyes on the road. "If he's smart, he'll try to take me instead of you."

I turned my head his way.

"Because he'll use me to get you to surrender."

And it would work.

"But we can't let that happen."

"No...we can't." The last thing I wanted was to be raped and tortured until someone finally killed me, but I would prefer that over something happening to Maverick. I'd rather be raped a million times than let anyone hurt him.

"If that ever does happen, don't do it."

"You know I would."

"But it would be a waste. He would get you out of hiding and kill me anyway. Trust me on that. That's how he plays."

I pulled one knee to my chest and looked out the window, taking comfort in the darkness that surrounded us. It was difficult to hide in a luscious landscape like this. Headlights were visible from a mile away.

Maverick was quiet for the rest of the drive home.

We pulled into the garage minutes later, then headed inside.

Now that I felt safe behind the walls along the perimeter and inside the stone structure of the house, I was exhausted. My body was so tense with discomfort because I'd spent all my energy being prepared for the seven-foot monster to jump out of nowhere.

I didn't bother going to my bedroom to change first. I headed straight for his bedroom and let him unzip the back of my dress. Once it came loose, I let it fall to the ground and then got into bed.

Maverick took his time pulling out his belongings from his pockets. His wallet sat on the dresser along with his watch. His phone came next. In clothes like that, he looked like one in a million. With beautiful golden skin and soft eyes made of caramel, he was as beautiful as he was delicious.

He stripped off his jacket and tossed it on the armchair then pulled his tie loose. Slowly, he unfastened each of the buttons on his collared shirt until he peeled it off and revealed a tight eight-pack with perfectly tanned skin. His body was so strong, practically bulletproof.

He loosened his belt and pushed his slacks down as he kicked off his shoes. Items of clothing fell to the floor until he stood in just his boxers, his thighs muscular and tight. Dark hair covered his calves and thighs, but it stopped at his waist. His torso was a smooth surface of muscle and skin.

His ass was the best part. It was tight and built like a brick house.

I could stare at his perfection all night long, watch it like it was a dirty movie.

But instead of it being fake, it was real…because he was the man I married.

He grabbed his phone and checked a few things before he made his way to the bed, his eyes still on his phone. He stopped at his nightstand, like he was prepared to put it down once he was finished reading whatever was on his screen.

I rose onto my knees then yanked down the front of his boxers, revealing a soft cock that was still impressive in its size.

He lowered his phone and looked down at me, his cock thickening instantaneously.

I put it between my lips and started to suck, feel it fill my mouth like an inflating balloon.

A quiet moan escaped his lips, and he tossed his phone onto the nightstand like he didn't give a damn.

On all fours with my ass in the air, I did my best, but his dick quickly became too big for my mouth so I only stuffed half of it inside. My tongue flattened, and I pushed it as deep as I could without causing my throat to gag. It was the first time I'd put his dick in my mouth, and I wasn't sure what had taken so long. I'd never been a fan of giving head, but I didn't mind doing this in the least. This was a cock that should be kissed, should be licked, should be eaten. It deserved it at all.

His hand moved into my hair, and he kept it out of my face as he watched me, transfixed by the way I sucked his big dick into my little mouth.

He got a little bigger and a little thicker, and tears sprang to my eyes because of the pressure on my throat. I struggled to breathe and keep my jaw unhinged like this, to arch my neck perfectly to suck his dick just right. The tears streaked down my face, just as they did when he made me come.

His hand cupped my cheek, and he brushed his thumb over my tear, smearing it across his finger as he watched me suck him off. He brought it to his mouth and tasted it, like he wanted to know how salty my tears were. "Look at me."

My eyes lifted to meet his as I kept sucking his dick. I stared at the beautiful man as he stood over me, as he watched me enjoy him so expressively. I wished I could take more of him, but this was all my anatomy could handle. He seemed to enjoy it all the same.

"You know how to suck dick."

Only when I felt like it.

He grabbed my neck and slowly pulled his dick out of my mouth. Once it left my tongue, it bounced down and hung between his legs, the veins thick and visible and the blood making his skin turn slightly red.

He pulled open his nightstand and grabbed a condom.

His black wedding ring sat there too, something he hadn't touched since our wedding day.

Then he shut the drawer again.

I was tired of using condoms. I was tired of feeling the latex separate us when we were monogamous. I wanted to feel this man come inside me, feel him fill me the way a husband should fill his wife.

But he rolled on the condom without thinking twice about it.

He got on top of me, widened my legs with his thighs, and then sank into me with an appreciative moan.

Once he was inside me, I stopped thinking about the layer between us. I just thought about him and those beautiful espresso eyes as they looked into mine. My hands were in his hair, and my lips were on his. Together, we moved our bodies, feeling each other and enjoying each other like there was nothing else in the world we would rather be doing. I breathed hard against his mouth as he picked up his pace, slamming into me good and hard. Soon, we were both covered in sweat, both lost in the clouds of desire.

"You feel so fucking good…" I grabbed his ass and pulled him deep inside me, thinking about Ruby's comment at the theater. She thought he was hot, just like everyone else. But I was his wife—the only woman in his bed. He was mine and no one else's.

He moaned as he pounded into me harder, his powerful legs keeping my knees apart. He panted with the exertion, his temples flushing red because he was consumed by the sex.

I'd never had sex this good with anyone else. It was either attributed to Maverick's bedroom skills…or he was the man I was most attracted to. It took two to tango, and we danced together so well, especially when he took the lead.

"I'm gonna come…" I gripped the back of his neck and felt my body tighten around him. His dick felt so much bigger when my pussy constricted in the explosion. It made clenching around his dick so much better, gripping it like I didn't want to let go.

"Yes, Sheep." He held his face above mine and watched me, sweat dripping from his forehead onto my skin. "Come for me."

After the way Kamikaze had assaulted me, I thought sex would be the last thing on my mind. But rape and sex were two different things, so they weren't related in my head. Making love to my husband was good and pure, borderline beautiful. It was so different that it couldn't be compared, being blanketed by affection from this man as he took me deep into the night. My nails dug into his ass as I finished, as I gushed around his cock with a climax that made my toes curl.

Once I was finished, he slowed down. He always brought things to a slower pace when he was about to explode. He wanted to make it last as long as possible, to enjoy the moment when he filled the tip of the condom with his ecstasy. With his gaze focused on mine, he gave his final pumps, his brown eyes filled with deep longing.

"Give it to me, Wolf." I wanted him to combust in a fiery explosion the way I did, to receive an enormous reward for all the work he'd just done. I wanted his body to go haywire, for his hips to buck automatically as the pleasure burst in every single vein. The only thing I wished was that there was nothing between us, that he would fill me with all the come that was about to go into that condom.

He rested his head against mine as he finished, as he grunted through the pleasure that made his back tighten. His dick thickened inside me, and he shuddered as the euphoria came to an end. He slowly softened on top of me, filling the condom and turning limp soon afterward. His face rested in my neck, and we breathed as our sweat smeared against each other's bodies.

My fingers moved into his hair and gently caressed the strands as I still felt him between my legs. I loved his weight on top of me, like a suit of armor that would deflect any bullet directed at me.

He finally got off and went into the bathroom to clean off.

I was still warm and sweaty, so I lay with the sheets kicked off, the moisture slowly evaporating from my skin.

He returned moments later, cold water splashed across his face. He turned off the lamp and got into bed beside me, sticking to his side because he was probably still hot. The dark surrounded us, enveloped us.

The shadows acting as a curtain, I tried to hide behind them as much as possible. "There's something I have to tell you..." I focused my gaze on the ceiling so I wouldn't have to see the anger corroding his face.

"What's your secret?"

"It's gonna make you angry."

He sighed in the darkness, his anger slowly replacing the sexy ambiance we'd just had a moment ago. "At least you're getting me prepared."

"I asked your sister to bring your father to the rehab center so I could talk to him. He was sitting in the dining room when I surprised him. I sat down, and we had a long chat..."

Maverick didn't give any reaction to what I said, but the silence was so damn loud. He could express so much disdain with so little effort. His anger made the temperature of the room rise a few degrees, slowly getting hotter until we both started to boil. He turned on his side and propped himself up, looking down at me with an expression that was more lethal than a bullet. "You went behind my back...again?"

"It wasn't like that."

"No, that's exactly what it was like." He didn't raise his voice, but he didn't need to. His anger was potent. "After all this time, do you really not understand how dangerous my father is? What he could have done to you?"

"He wasn't armed—"

"He doesn't need to be armed to kill you. His bare hands are more than enough."

In hindsight, it did feel stupid...especially with everything else that followed. "I tried to repair your relationship with him. I told him how sorry I was about his wife... I told him you wanted to have a better relationship with him."

Maverick rolled his eyes. "That's the dumbest thing you could have said to him."

"Yeah, I realize that now."

"He doesn't give a shit about that. All he cares about is what he wants—which is killing you."

Obviously.

"You provoked him, and his response was to tattle on me to Kamikaze. I won't hand you over, so he's letting that psychopath do his dirty work. This is why you don't do shit without my authorization." He got out of bed and gripped his skull. "You think you know better, but you don't know a damn thing—"

"That's not why I did it. I just wanted you to get your father back—"

"And that's never going to happen. I know that better than anyone." He opened the bedroom door. "Get out, Arwen."

I sat up in bed, shocked that he wanted me to leave when I was buck naked and still sweaty.

He kept his hand on the door. "Go."

"I don't want to go."

"I don't give a shit. You went behind my back a second time—"

"I was trying to help—"

"You trying to help is going to get you raped and me killed." He grabbed me by the wrist and yanked me out of bed. "With all the shit I've done for you, this is how you repay me? You do realize that I would die for you, right?"

I faced him as the tears welled up in my eyes. "I'm so sorry…"

"That's not enough. An apology is just an admission of wrongdoing."

"That's not what my apology means. I didn't mean to hurt you. I was just trying to help you—"

"Get out." He dropped his chin and stared at the floor, like he didn't want to look at me a second longer.

I didn't step into the hallway. This bedroom was my sanctuary. This man was my protector. My bedroom was all the way on the other side of the house, and that was too far. "Please let me stay with you... You're the only reason I can sleep at night."

With one hand on his hip, he continued to stand there and look down at the ground. His chest rose and fell with his deep breathing because he was continuing to combat the rage.

I stayed put. "I don't want to leave you... Don't make me go."

Something I said must have changed his mind because he shut the door. Without looking at me, he walked back to bed. His heavy body fell on the sheets, and he lay there, his eyes on the ceiling.

I returned to bed and gave him his space. I wanted to cuddle into his side and apologize again, but I knew he didn't want to hear it. The only reason he'd let me stay was because I practically begged.

He didn't have the heart to kick me out when he knew I was scared.

I turned on my side and looked at him, knowing he would never meet my gaze. "I thought if I put your family back together...you would be happy."

He was quiet. With his eyes on the ceiling and a still body, he seemed oblivious to what I said. "The only way you can put my family back together is if you bring my mother back from the dead. My father only cares about her, not the rest of us."

It seemed that way, but I couldn't believe that was really true.

"I'm trying to keep the promise I made to your father. But if you keep undermining me, that's never going to happen. You say we're a team, but you never act like it. You take matters into your own hands like you have some master plan that's going to save us all. You're just a stupid girl who doesn't understand a goddamn thing. Know your place."

Those words stung because I'd heard them before—from his father's lips. In his anger, he was just like the man who raised him. They possessed the same heartless coldness, the same harshness. "Maverick." I reached across the bed and rested my fingertips against his arm. "I don't remember exactly when it happened, but something is different between us. There's something here, a bond deeper than friendship and desire. We care about each other very much, would easily take a bullet for each other. There's been no other man in my bed because you're the only person that I want…and I know you feel the same way."

"What's your point?" he asked coldly.

"My point is…I had good intentions. It doesn't make it right. Doesn't make me less ill-advised. But I was trying to help you, trying to take the most diplomatic approach. I was doing it for you…because you mean everything to me. I'll never do anything behind your back again."

"You've said that before."

"But now I really mean it. You and I…we're a team." I rested my hand on his and hoped he would reciprocate my affection.

But his hand lay there, lifeless.

"It's you and I…forever." Now, I wasn't married to his man

because I had to be. I was married to him because I wanted to be. There was no other man I could picture spending my life with. No other man could compare to what I already had. I wanted Kamikaze to be killed and Caspian to disappear. With our enemies out of the way, it could just be us…together.

When I least expected it, his fingers came to life and squeezed my hand.

And I squeezed his back.

## 14

## MAVERICK

I STUDIED THE WAY SHE HELD THE GUN. HER FINGERS GRIPPED the handle, but she was so inexperienced that it was tilted slightly sideways. If she pulled the trigger, she would miss the target by several feet. "Like this." I grabbed her wrist and righted it.

"I'm not that bad, am I?"

"When I walked into the apartment, you pointed that gun at me with the safety on. If I could tell, so could he." I guided her fingers to hit the button and turn off the safety. "Always have this on when the gun is in your purse or on your hip. But don't forget to turn it off the second you draw it."

She aimed the gun at the red target in the field. The cows were in the barn, so they wouldn't run off and accidentally get hit.

I grabbed her elbow and straightened her arm. "Use your other hand to support you." I placed her other hand on the gun. I'd been using guns since I was fifteen years old, so it was so obvious to me when someone couldn't handle one. "When you fire, there will be a bit of a kickback. Shoot."

She closed one eye and tried to aim closer in on her target, her shoulders tight and her posture rigid.

I stepped back, already knowing the outcome before she even pulled the trigger.

Her fingers squeezed the trigger—and she missed. The loud bang reverberated over the land of my estate, like an echo that could shatter eardrums. The cows started to moo in the barn, hearing the sound just as well as we could.

I came back to her side. "Keep the gun steady. If you shake, the second you pull the trigger, you're never going to hit anything."

"They make it look so easy in the movies..."

"It is easy. You just have to know what you're doing." I helped her set up once more. "Again." I stepped back.

She aimed once more. This time, she hit the target—but at the very edge.

I came back to her and tilted her head. "If you focus on the circle here, it'll help you hit your mark."

"I never see you use it."

"When you get the hang of it, you don't need it. Guns like these are used for close range. When a guy is standing right in front of you, you should be able to hit him without aiming." I moved several feet behind her.

She kept shooting, emptying the barrel as her bullets flew

through the air. She finally hit the target every time—and even got a bull's-eye.

"Reload." I came to her side and handed her the ammo.

She grabbed the box and pointed the gun down to access the barrel.

"Aren't you forgetting something?"

"What?"

I hit the button for the safety. "Always turn that on if you aren't using it—especially when you're loading ammo while the gun is pointed at your feet."

---

I WAS CAUGHT up at work, but I chose to sit in my office just to be out of the house.

I was still pissed at my wife.

Even if she meant well, she still tiptoed around behind my back. Nothing I hated more than a stupid person thinking they were smart. She was idiotic for thinking she could approach my father for a heartfelt one-on-one conversation.

She really thought it would be that simple?

I sat at my desk and enjoyed a cigar while I looked out the window. I'd trained Arwen to use a gun, and she was proficient enough to be able to kill someone who charged her at close range.

At least she had a resource if I wasn't around.

I had every right to be upset and kick her out of my bedroom, but when she'd asked to stay, I couldn't refuse.

This woman made me so fucking soft.

Maybe my father was right. I really was weak.

It was embarrassing to have your wife fight your battles for you, to admit I had a broken heart and I missed the way my family used to be.

Pussy shit.

Of course, my father didn't care.

I leaned back in the leather chair and kept smoking, letting the nicotine calm my body. I still hadn't figured out what to do about Kamikaze. Would I round up every man I had and provoke him into uncharted territory? That seemed stupid.

But waiting for him to ambush me was stupider.

There was a real possibility Kamikaze would kill me and Arwen would become a slave.

Death wasn't what I feared most—it was the latter.

Kamikaze respected me, so he would make the kill clean. He would just shoot me in between the eyes and put me down. There would be no torture or humiliation. For a psychopath, he could be pragmatic at times. My fate would be far more bearable than what Arwen would have to suffer through.

That was why I had to win.

For her.

But how did you defeat a man like him? We had become allies because it would be stupid to be enemies. Our Italian blood ran deep in the soil, back several generations. There was mutual respect for our culture. He did illegal shit; I did illegal shit. But we kept our mouths shut and looked the other way.

But then Arwen's father ruined all of that.

This never would have happened if my father hadn't forced me to marry her. We never would have met, so her fate wouldn't have mattered to me. People were tortured and killed every day. It was irrelevant.

But even if I could back in time and change things…I wouldn't.

"So much for working late."

I turned around and saw Arwen standing in the doorway, her arms crossed over her chest with threat in her eyes. She glanced at the cigar sitting between my fingertips then looked at me with a promise of punishment.

She sauntered into the room and approached my desk. In jeans and a t-shirt, she was prepared for the cool breeze outside the house. Fall was deepening, and now summer was just a memory.

She snatched the cigar out of my hand. "What did we talk about?"

"You're going to berate me for smoking, but you're the one who snuck behind my back and cornered my father?" I took the cigar back and placed it between my lips. "I'm the only thing standing between you and Kamikaze. If I want to smoke, I'll fucking smoke." I puffed heavily, refusing to participate in this husband and wife routine. She really did feel like the lady of the house.

"If you want to live, you won't." She pulled the cigar out of my mouth and stabbed it in the ashtray.

I had all the power in the relationship. I could backhand her across the face and kick her out of my office. I could do anything I wanted, and she would have no power to stop me. But I let her boss me around, let her take away my cigars like she owned me.

"Keep drinking. But stop smoking."

"Life is short. If the smoke doesn't kill me, something else will."

"And what if something else doesn't?" she questioned. "I need you to live a long and healthy life."

"Why? With me gone, you would inherit an immense amount of wealth."

She tilted her head slightly, offended by that statement. "I would rather be poor with you by my side than live in that mansion alone." Her sincerity was obvious in the tone of her voice, the way she held my gaze with hurt in her eyes.

My father thought I was weak. My sister lived in a different reality. Arwen seemed to be the only person who cared about me for me—with all my good qualities and my flaws. It didn't seem to matter what I did; her affection was unconditional.

"No more smoking, Maverick. I mean it." She opened the top drawer of my desk and found my stash of cigars. She

*The Wolf and His Wife*

grabbed them and dumped them in the scotch sitting beside me.

I stared at the damage then looked back at her. "That's €5,000 scotch."

"Then it really taught you a lesson." She leaned toward me, gripping the back of my chair for support. "Don't let me catch you smoking again. I promise you'll regret it."

I stared into her eyes and watched the fire dance. When I got lost in the beauty of her face, I forgot how much she'd just pissed me off, how she'd destroyed my cigars and my prized booze. All I could think about was the sexy curve of her bottom lip, the way I'd kissed it just the night before. This woman infuriated me, but she somehow earned my respect at the same time.

She straightened and dropped her hand from the chair. "When are you coming home?"

"When I finish my drink and cigar."

"Well, I took care of that." She crossed her arms over her chest.

"Then I guess I'm coming home now." I pushed the chair back and rose to my feet, my height towering over her petite size.

She tilted her chin automatically to meet my gaze. Her long brown hair was a curtain around her shoulders, and her white t-shirt set off the beautiful color of her eyes. Even when she wasn't in a ball gown singing her heart out to her admirers, she was still absolutely stunning.

She planted her hand against my chest and rose onto her

tiptoes, slowly bringing her lips to mine. When they came together, she gave me the softest kiss, her lips tasting like red wine. She closed her eyes while she enjoyed it, then pulled away.

Kissing her felt natural. Kissing was usually the prelude to sex, but with Arwen, it wasn't necessarily the prelude to anything. Sometimes, it happened...just to happen. And it felt good all on its own even if it didn't develop into something more. It was about the affection, the connection.

She pulled her hand away from my chest. "I hope you aren't still mad at me."

"You know how stubborn I am."

"Yes...but I also know how forgiving you are."

"When have I ever been forgiving?"

"You've forgiven me once. You let your father live because you still see the good in him...even if it's not there. You're a lot more compassionate than you give yourself credit for, Maverick."

I'd held that gun to his forehead, and I didn't pull the trigger. That was a sign of weakness, not compassion. "That's not a good thing."

She interlocked our fingers then guided me out of the office. "I disagree."

---

Without waiting for permission, she made herself at home in my bedroom.

*The Wolf and His Wife*

She left her clothes and accessories in her room on the other side of the house, but she helped herself to my bed every night—like it was half hers.

I sat up in bed and scrolled through my phone when she walked inside. Sometimes I thought I should object to the direction this relationship was going. It started off casual, but now it actually felt like a marriage. We were a man and a woman who slept together every single night. I never verbally agreed to that. It just happened.

I didn't mind it. But I didn't like the position it put me in.

I lifted my gaze from my phone, not prepared for what I was about to see.

In an open silk robe, she stood wearing black lingerie with garters on her thighs. Little black bows adorned the silk of her thong and bra, and her dark makeup made her look ready for a photo shoot.

My phone slipped from my grasp and landed in my lap.

She sauntered farther into the room, her eyes locked on me like I was the only man in her thoughts. She approached the bed because I was immobile, still surprised at what I was witnessing.

I didn't see lingerie often. My flings were too short for that kind of planning.

She pulled the robe off her shoulders, and it slipped to the floor. Then she pushed her black thong over her hips and let it slide down her legs until it joined the other article of clothing. Her pussy was perfectly shaved, her cute clit ready for my pelvic bone.

I was still rigid because I couldn't process what I was looking at. My cock practically pierced my boxers, and my throat ran dry because she was so stunning. She had the perfect body to show off that lingerie.

She climbed onto the bed then straddled my hips, my boxers at my thighs so she could slowly sink down until I was perfectly situated inside her. Her hands reached behind her back and unclasped her bra. When the material was gone and her tits were on display, she really looked phenomenal.

I stared at her tits before my eyes flicked up to lock on hers again.

"I want to show you how sorry I am…" She palmed against my chest and sat directly on my dick, her soft slit smearing my length with her slickness.

I closed my eyes because it felt so good, to feel bare pussy like that. I'd never been with a woman without a condom, only fingered them. Feeling just a bead of her arousal was like a drop of heaven.

Her arms circled my neck, and she pressed her tits against my chest, her hard nipples dragging lightly against me. Her mouth was close to mine, her soft lips desperate for my kiss.

I had the most beautiful woman on my lap—and she was my wife. "I forgive you…"

"I haven't even done anything yet," she whispered against my mouth.

My hands squeezed her hips, and a shiver ran up my spine. "That's how good you are."

## The Wolf and His Wife

My driver pulled up to the entrance of the theater, and I got out of the car, taking Arwen's hand so I could help her to her feet. She was in a stunning black dress, the fabric hugging her sexy frame perfectly.

I pulled her close and guided her up the stairs.

"It'll be nice to go to the theater without performing in it." Covered in diamonds and looking every bit like a DeVille, she was my crown jewel. Her hair was in tight curls, and she had it pinned back to show off her perfect face.

"Don't be surprised if they ask you to sing at some point."

"And I'll oblige…because they won't take no."

The usher guided us to the private box where I was meeting the guys. The show had already begun, so we greeted each other quietly then took our seats.

Her hand immediately went to my thigh, her wedding ring shining in the darkness.

My hand rested on top of hers, and I glanced at her beside me. She was already focused on the stage, her eyes reflecting the bright lights. A slight smile was on her lips as she immediately became absorbed in the story.

She didn't notice me looking at her, so I continued to enjoy my vantage point. The light hit her cheeks perfectly, showing off the beautiful contours of her face. Her bow-shaped lips were phenomenal in that red lipstick. She outshone all the actors onstage, dulled the beauty of the other women.

When she worked for my forgiveness, she got more than just that.

The show was over an hour later, and the lights came on as we rose to our feet. Now, proper introductions were made. I introduced my wife to the few people who hadn't met her yet, and everyone else who did know her was thrilled to see her once more.

We were escorted to a private room in the back of the theater, a fancy dining hall where the aristocrats used to have their private meals after the conclusion of the show. High-top tables were everywhere, and large windows gave prime views of the city. Waiters passed with glasses of champagne and trays appetizers.

She sipped her champagne and watched the occupancy of the room rise, more people from our party joining us. "I never expected a man like you to attend so many parties. You seem like someone who would be home every single night if he had the choice."

"Networking is the most important aspect of business." It was how I got eighty percent of my business, just from a mere introduction. Other acquaintances vouched for me, and then my credibility was established. "But you're right." I took a sip of my champagne. "I hate this shit."

"Good thing you have me. I think I'm a little more approachable."

She was definitely my better half. "A lot more, actually." My arm curled around her waist as more people came up to us for a chitchat. Everyone recognized her from the opera because going to the theater was the biggest hobby for most of them. They got lost in conversation, and naturally, I was forgotten.

I didn't mind. If I could be a fly on the wall, I would be.

I excused myself to get another drink, but I never made it to the bar.

Standing in the corner making small talk with someone was the seven-foot asshole I hated.

His eyes shifted to mine, and he raised his glass like he was giving a toast. His pearly white teeth reflected the light from the chandelier. They were so bright, it was obvious they weren't real. He'd had dentures put in his mouth long ago after all his teeth got punched out.

He was probably armed, but so was I.

I remained calm and didn't seem the least bit offended by his presence. I continued to the bar, ordered my drink like everything was fine, and then made my way over just as his guest stepped away.

"Nice party." His flute of champagne was particularly small in his large grasp. He downed it until it was empty then placed it on a passing tray. His hands slid into his pockets as he surveyed the guests at the party.

Knowing he was only twenty feet from my wife made my blood boil. I knew what he'd tried to do to her, how he intended to use her to line his pockets with gold. The anger was so paramount that I was motionless. All I could do was stare at him. The second I reached for my gun, he would reach for his—and a lot of people would die.

"Your wife looks good in diamonds."

"Because she is a diamond."

He chuckled. "That's a good way to put it."

"What's your plan? Take her in front of three hundred people?"

"No. If I made a scene, I would never get invited again."

How did he get invited to begin with? "I have a feeling you weren't given an invitation in the first place."

He smiled, showing his obnoxiously white teeth. "Just talk like you're rich, and people think you're rich. That's all you have to do to survive at these hoity-toity social parties." When another waiter walked by, he snapped his fingers to get his attention then took a drink off the tray. "Then you can have all the free food and booze you want."

"I doubt you're in a position where you need free anything."

"I don't know…Arwen's father hit me pretty hard. The bank repossessed his homes and antiques, so I was left with nothing." Now that the subject had been broached, it turned hostile. His eyes were on me, full of warning. My instinct was to get Arwen out of there, but being surrounded by three hundred people was the safest place she could be. And since I was there, I could keep eyes on him at all times. "Maverick, I don't want it to be this way. You and your father are good men." His hand moved to my shoulder, and he squeezed like we were old friends.

I pushed off his hand. "Touch me again, and I'll stab that flute into your neck."

He brushed off the threat like it was of no consequence at all. "We both know how this is going to go. A lot of men are going to die. A lot of resources will be wasted. If we spend too much time focused on each other, we won't notice what our other enemies are doing. I've already offered to pay you generously. So, take the money, and let's end this."

He could offer me a billion dollars, and I still wouldn't be tempted. "You could make me king of the world, and I still would turn you down."

He shook his head slightly, like he was disappointed. "The butcher should never get too close to the livestock. Rule number one, Maverick."

"I promised her father I would keep her safe in exchange for the information. I have to fulfill that promise."

"But he has to fulfill his promise to me." Now that the conversation had deepened, his mood soured. He poked his finger to his chest as he stepped closer and leered down at me. "He made me that promise first. I get priority."

"She had nothing to do with that."

"Boo-hoo." He finished his drink then left the glass on the end table like an asshole. "Her father is dead, so what does it matter?"

"It matters because I keep my word."

He studied me as his features softened. "That has nothing to do with this, and we both know it. You have to ask yourself if you're willing to deal with this headache for a piece of ass. Don't forget that's all she is—just a piece of ass."

She'd never been that to me. "Let this go, Kamikaze. You have a million ways to make money."

"But I shouldn't have to. She should make the money for me."

She may be my sheep, but she was no animal. "I don't want men to die for this war. I don't want to use my ammo for this stupidity. But I'll do it if you force me. I'll do whatever it takes to protect her. If that's how it has to be, that's how it has to be." Now, the conflict had been established, and there was nothing left to do but fight. We were officially enemies. The crowded room didn't make me feel any safer than if we were alone in a dark field.

Kamikaze shook his head slightly. "That's unfortunate, Maverick. That means one of us will live—and one of us will die."

"Doesn't have to be that way. Just let it go."

"I won't let it go just as much as you won't," he said bitterly. "But I want to minimize my losses. I've got a lot of other shit to worry about. So, this is my proposal."

I already knew what was coming.

"Russian roulette—you and me."

My eyes glanced higher and noticed the scar on that was visible through his hair. A bullet had torn through his skull and became buried in his brain. Somehow, the motherfucker had survived. But he wouldn't survive it again.

If we played the game and I got the bullet, I hoped I would be as lucky.

But probably not.

"You're a man of your word, Maverick. So, should we agree

on a time and a place? Or would you rather do this the old-fashioned way?"

He had just as many resources as I did. It would be a battle resulting in many casualties. I was equally likely to die from a stray bullet. When it came to clashes like that, there was always one victor and one loser.

This option minimized the bullshit.

I glanced at Arwen on the other side of the room. Oblivious to the conversation we were having, she laughed with her companion and continued to enjoy the fresh glass of champagne that had been placed in her hand. Was this woman really worth my own life? I could hand her over right now, and the whole thing would be over. I turned my gaze back to him once my mind was made up. "Let's do it tomorrow."

## 15

## ARWEN

Maverick was quiet for the rest of the night. He only said a few words to his acquaintances. With a glass always pressed to his lips, he spent the evening drinking. He ditched the flutes of champagne and went straight for the liquor.

Just like last time, everyone asked me to sing a song. I sat at the piano and played a new song I'd written just weeks ago. When I looked at Maverick, he wasn't paying attention. He stood at the window and looked out at the street, indifferent to my song.

A switch had flipped in his head.

We said goodbye to everyone and then got inside the car waiting at the curb. The driver pulled away and took us to the estate in Florence. I wanted to ask what was bothering him, but since we had no privacy, I stayed quiet.

He stuck to his side of the car and didn't blanket me with affection. He was so cold, it didn't seem like I was there at all. His thoughts plagued him and dragged him to the bottom of the deepest lake.

Twenty minutes later, we entered the house. It was late and Abigail was already asleep. This place had felt like a prison when I first arrived here, but now it was the most beautiful home I'd ever been in. Just the entryway alone was marvelous, with ceilings so high I could barely make out the chandelier at the top when the lights were off.

"What's bothering you?" We took the stairs, side by side. I lifted up my gown so my heels could rise onto the next step without snagging on anything.

He ignored my question.

"You were fine when we got there, but now you're dead inside."

We made it to the second landing then turned to go up the third. With one hand in his pocket and his shoulders slouched, he didn't seem to hear me. His thoughts were a million miles away, still focused on the subject that had stolen all his attention.

I made it to the third landing then dropped my dress. "Maverick."

He walked ahead of me and entered his bedroom. He pushed the door open and immediately slipped off his jacket and set it on the armchair. His fingers popped open his shirt buttons, and then he pulled that off too. The tie landed on the floor.

My heels were killing me, so I slipped them off. "What's going on?"

He loosened his belt then fell into the armchair. He was bare-chested with tight abs, and his eyes were heavy from all the liquor he ingested. The top button on his pants was popped open, and some of his happy trail was visible.

If I weren't so alarmed by his behavior, I would sink to my knees and suck him dry.

With his fingertips resting against his temple, he watched me. "Kamikaze was there tonight."

That simple sentence was enough to explain everything. My chest tightened in terror, and my heart started to race with unease. He had been in the same room with me, somehow hidden among the three hundred faces enjoying themselves at the party. He was seven feet tall, so I had no idea how I'd missed him.

"He and I had a chat."

The man turned up when we least expected it. Maverick obviously had no idea he would be there. Otherwise, he wouldn't have brought me. A man so big could still be so sneaky. My fingers reached to the back of my dress, and I pulled down the zipper because my gown suddenly felt too tight.

"I tried to talk some sense into him…but that's not possible." His eyes shifted away, and he looked at the empty fireplace. He stared at it without blinking.

I crossed my arms over my chest, feeling a sudden draft.

"We decided to settle this tomorrow." He dropped his fingers from his temple and finally looked at me for the first time. He seemed defeated, overwhelmed, and even a little resentful.

"What does that mean?"

He pushed against the wooden armrests and rose to his feet. "Russian roulette."

It was worse than having Kamikaze storm the gates and try to kill everyone. This precisely laid out the odds, so I knew how likely it was that Maverick would survive. It was all dependent on the position of one bullet in one chamber—and when he pulled the trigger. "No...you can't do this."

"I have no choice." He stood in front of me, his chin tilted down so he could look me in the eye.

"Yes, you do. This can't be the best option. You said you would kill him and—"

"The odds of survival are the same. He's got a ton of men, and so do I. We're just going to kill a bunch of people and waste our resources to settle this. I tried to convince him to let this go, but he refused. He's not going to stop until he has you."

"Well, I'm not letting you do this. I'm not letting you play this sick game for me." I couldn't imagine the two of them sitting across from each other at a table and taking turns putting guns to their foreheads. With every click of the gun, Maverick would be a little closer to getting the bullet. "I would much rather hand myself over—"

"And I'd rather you not." He stepped closer to me, his eyes full of determination. "I'd rather die than let that happen to you."

"But if you die, then it happens to me anyway. Your life isn't worth that, Maverick. I would never want that to happen to you—"

*The Wolf and His Wife*

"I have a plan to get you out of there."

"What's the point if you're dead?" Tears cascaded down my cheeks, and my voice kept escalating higher and higher. "No. We aren't doing this. I won't allow you to do this for me. Even my father wouldn't want you to."

His voice dropped. "I'm not doing it for him."

"But still..."

"If Kamikaze gets the bullet, our problems are solved. He'll be gone for good."

"What if he survives again?"

"Doesn't matter. The decision will still be made. And there's no way that guy is going to survive a second bullet to the head."

"Maverick, I don't like this—"

"And I don't care." He stepped away from me then pushed off his slacks. His shoes came next, then he stood in just his black boxers. "This is how we're settling this."

"That's outrageous—"

"It's the only option we have."

"How do you know he won't trick you? Put a bullet in every chamber of the barrel and make you go first?"

"Someone will show us the barrel. He may be a psychopath, but he's not a cheat."

My fingers shoved into my hair, making my perfectly styled hair frizz as I dragged my hands down my face. I smeared my tears against my skin, ruined my expertly applied makeup.

"This matter will never be settled until he's dead or I'm dead. I don't want to talk about this anymore." He turned to the bed and pulled back the covers. It might be his last night on earth, but he acted like his doom didn't await him. How could he be so calm about the worst night of his life?

"That's too bad because we aren't done talking."

He leaned against the pillow and looked at me, his eyes full of lethal warning. "I won't change my mind. You don't understand my world the way I do. Without my father's army to help me, I'm just as likely to die anyway. Kamikaze is not a man you want to fight. This is the simplest solution."

"Letting me surrender is the simplest solution. I would much rather do that than let—"

"And I wouldn't. He's just as likely to get the bullet as I am. It's an even match."

"But every time someone pulls that trigger, your chances get worse."

"And so do his." He got out of bed again and walked up to me. "Nothing you say is going to change my mind. I know how much you like to sneak around behind my back, but you aren't going to hand yourself over to him. The gates are locked, and you aren't getting through."

That was exactly what I would have done—but he was too smart for that.

"Now, let me get some sleep."

"You can actually close your eyes and drift off right now?"

The two bullet wounds were noticeable in his shoulder. Old scars that would never truly heal, they blemished his perfect skin, but they also added character. This man was a soldier, a fighter. He'd promised to protect me, and he kept that vow —even when no one else would. "I'm pretty drunk. So, yes." He turned back to the bed and got under the covers. The lamp was clicked off, and he lay there, his body relaxing into the mattress.

I stood there as my loose dress began to slip off my shoulders. The night had started off so grand, a social event with champagne and good company. My husband was the most handsome man in the room—and I felt lucky to be on his arm. But now, the good things in my life had come to an end —snuffed out like a lit candle.

I stared at his exhausted form on the bed and felt my heart clench from the pain. A life without him wasn't a life worth living. He was more than just the man I'd been forced to marry. He really was my husband now. He was the man I wanted in my arms as well as in my bed.

I slipped off the dress then got into bed, only wearing my panties even though there would be no sex tonight. He was too drunk, and I was too depressed. It was obvious Maverick was worried about tomorrow because he'd drowned himself in so much booze, he wouldn't have to think about it. His life was held in the balance by chance. All that mattered was where that bullet was in the barrel.

Maybe he really didn't have other options. But his defeat reminded me of the afternoon when his father stormed into the house and tried to kill him. Maverick had pretty much rolled over and allowed it to happen—as if he wanted his father to kill him.

It was obvious depression was a major component of his character. Dealing with his mother's terrible death, his sister's illness, and his father's hatred was enough to make him give up on everything.

Maybe he felt like he had nothing to lose.

I lay beside him and watched his face. His expression restful and calm, it didn't seem like he cared what would happen tomorrow. Forfeiting his life was easy because he didn't have anything to lose. He would rather die to save me than live his life to the fullest.

Even though he didn't want my affection, I scooted closer to him and laid my arm across his stomach. My face rested next to his, my lips touching his shoulder. After a deep breath that made me shudder, tears welled up in my eyes then streaked down my cheeks. My fingers tightened against his skin, and I held my breath to keep the sobs at bay. "I can't lose you…"

---

I DIDN'T SLEEP that night.

I kept clinging to Maverick like it was the last time we would ever be together. This man had become my whole world, and not just because he took care of me. He was my friend, my lover, my everything.

When he woke up the next morning, his eyes weren't filled with as much intoxication, but it was obvious he was a bit hungover. He sat up in bed then ran his fingers through his hair. After he glanced at the clock on the nightstand to check the time, he looked at me. As if everything had rushed back into his brain, his eyes hardened with the event that would take place today. "You didn't sleep."

"No." I sat up and kissed his shoulder, wanting to drown this man in kisses. I wanted to feel him beside me every night until time claimed our bodies. I didn't want to lose him to a bully on steroids.

He turned his face toward mine then placed a kiss on my upper cheek, his lips brushing past my messy hair. Then he slipped out of the bed and got to his feet. With a muscular back and powerful thighs, he looked like a gladiator without his armor. He stretched his arms over his head, his back rippling in response. As if it was an ordinary day with ordinary events on the calendar, he walked into the bathroom and got his day started.

I lay back on the pillow and stared at the ceiling—sick to my stomach.

---

HE WALKED down the stairs to the dining room, dressed in jeans and a t-shirt with a gun on his hip.

I followed him. "You're just going to act like everything is normal?"

"How else am I supposed to act?" He reached the bottom of the stairs and then entered the dining room. Breakfast was already laid out, omelets with coffee. He took a seat and filled his mug, like he was about to go to work the second he was finished.

I sat across from him, flabbergasted he could be so calm. "Like this might be your last day on earth."

He took another drink. "People die every day. I'm going to die just like everyone else. Whether it happens now or in thirty years doesn't make a difference."

"It makes a *huge* difference."

He shrugged. "Everyone has different opinions about death. I don't have an opinion. I just accept it."

"How can you talk like that? How can you be okay with all of this? This isn't even your fault—"

"We can argue about it all day, or we can just enjoy our breakfast. If I really do only have a few hours left, this isn't how I want to spend them." He grabbed his cloth napkin and pulled the silverware from the interior. With hunched shoulders, he leaned forward and shoveled the food into his mouth.

It would be easy to admire him for his bravery, but I knew his courage stemmed from a dark place. "You aren't afraid to die because you want to die…"

He stopped eating and lifted his eyes.

With heartbreak in my veins, I held his gaze and felt my heart sink into my stomach.

"I'm not suicidal."

"No…but you don't want to keep living either."

He turned his eyes back to his food and kept eating. "Sometimes, I get tired. There's so much bad and very little good. And the good things that happen to you don't last forever. Then you're haunted by the memories."

I knew he was referring to his perfect family. Everything was great...until it wasn't. "You still have a lot to live for... I want you to live."

"But I would rather die than let something happen to you. I have to protect my people too. If I let us shoot it out, Abigail would get hurt, along with other people I care about. This is clean and has dignity. And you keep assuming I'm going to lose."

"The odds aren't great, Maverick..."

"They're good enough if you ask me." He stabbed his fork into his food and placed it in his mouth. "I've been a part of this world my entire life. I know how these things go. You've been sheltered and oblivious for the last twentysomething years. This is a difficult pill to swallow, but you need to be strong."

"Maverick...I can't lose you." I repeated the same words to him that I'd whispered last night. "You mean everything to me now. This started off as a nightmare, but everything has changed. You're my husband, and you're supposed to take care of me. But I'm your wife, and I'm supposed to take care of you too—"

"That wasn't the deal. I take care of you—"

"It's the deal now. There has to be another way..."

He stared at his plate then shook his head. "There is no other way, Sheep."

"You could give me to him..." I didn't want to be a slave to that man. He would rape me, along with all his other men. Then assholes would pay big money to fuck me. I'd get knocked around, and my existence would be so terrible, I'd wish for death. But it was still better than watching Maverick shoot himself in the head.

His eyes narrowed like I'd just offended him down to his core. His shoulders tightened, and the affectionate mood in the room was quickly wiped away and replaced by rage. When he tightened his jaw, I knew my suggestion wasn't taken. "Never."

The breath I was holding escaped my lips. "Why? Why would you risk your life for me?"

He held my gaze, his dark eyes matching the black liquid inside his mug. A full minute passed, and all he did was stare, his eyes shifting back and forth slightly because they were too intense to stay still. "The same reason you would risk yours for mine."

---

HE SAT on the couch across from me, a cigar in between his lips. His large shoulders leaned against the back of the seat while the smoke drifted from his mouth. His eyes were tilted to the window behind his desk, and they reflected the autumn sunlight as his mind turned over his thoughts.

Since it might be his last day alive, I didn't scold him for the cigar.

In fact, I lit up myself. "When is this happening?"

"Not sure."

"So, this could happen anytime?"

His phone vibrated in his front pocket, and he fished it out. With his eyes on the screen, he said, "We're about to find out." He took the call and pressed it to his ear. "Chickened out?"

I was flabbergasted he could answer the phone so nonchalantly. A loaded gun would be pointed at his temple in just a few hours. With a simple squeeze, that bullet could be in his brain and his mind would be lost forever.

Kamikaze's voice was audible because it was so loud and deep. "Nah. I'm looking forward to this. How about your barn?"

"Neutral turf."

"Alright. How about Giovanni's place?"

"That works for me."

Was that a person? Or a restaurant?

"Let's meet in an hour," Kamikaze said. "Unless you've decided to chicken out."

I wanted to grab the phone and offer to hand myself over, but it wouldn't make a difference.

Maverick was just as calm now as he was before the phone rang. Relaxed on the couch with a thick cigar in his hand, he seemed like he could fall asleep because he was surrounded by peace. "I'm feeling pretty lucky today."

Kamikaze chuckled. "That makes two of us, Maverick. And I want her there. The second you're dead, I'm gonna bend her over the table and fuck her while you lie dead on the floor."

## 16

## MAVERICK

Was I scared?

No.

Was I lying?

No.

I had a plan set to get Arwen out of there if things went south. But if she didn't escape, at least I wouldn't be alive to witness the pain of her torment. I would cease to exist—which meant I wouldn't suffer anymore.

In a twisted way, I looked forward to the game we were about to play. If I won, it would solve all my problems. Arwen could lead a full life without looking over her shoulder, and I would never have to deal with that giant again.

I was risking a lot—but I could also gain a lot.

She was shocked by the calm way I approached the dilemma, and her assumption was right. I wasn't afraid to die—because I was tired of living. When my mother perished, so did my entire family. I felt like the last of my bloodline. My father had pulled me into a dark underworld I never should have been a part of. If he hadn't, Mother would still be alive. Lily would be happy. My father would still be the same man.

Now, he was a stranger.

The only family I had left was my wife—but sometimes that wasn't enough.

Before we left, I locked the door to my office and made the call. I already knew how the conversation would go, what I would say and what he would say in return. I could predict the entire exchange, down to the scoffs and laughs. But I called anyway...hoping I would be wrong.

He answered. "Didn't expect to hear from you."

So, he had no idea what was about to happen. "Kamikaze and I are about to play Russian roulette. The victor gets Arwen. Just thought you should know I might be dead in thirty minutes." There was still a piece of my old soul inside me, the boy who looked up to his father. I was a grown man with a lot of accomplishments, but I still needed the validation from the man I'd admired. It was twisted.

He was quiet—which was expected.

I had expected more than just his silence. "If I die, this is on you." He'd stabbed me in the back when he ratted me out to Kamikaze, which was disgusting, considering he'd made me marry her in the first place. I actually wanted to die so the guilt would fester inside him until it opened a wound in his stomach.

"You're forgetting your other option."

"Do you want me to take that option because you actually give a damn? Or just so you can get your revenge?"

He turned quiet again.

"I'm not giving her up. She's my wife—and I'd die for her." I didn't want to be disappointed further, so I ended the call and crushed the phone in my fingers. I stared at the wall, ignoring the historical painting my art dealer found for me. Every aspect of this room was tailored to my mood so it was a safe haven, but that comfort couldn't chase away my feelings. It couldn't chase away the hatred that burned in my heart.

---

ARWEN SAT RIGHT beside me in the back seat on the drive, her hand gripping mine as the tears continued to stream down her cheeks. She would calm herself enough to still them, but then minutes later, they returned. She was a spectrum of emotions, a wide variety of sadness.

Her arm linked through mine, and she held my hand on her thigh. She'd finally stopped trying to change my mind about my decision, especially now that we were only ten minutes away. I was a stubborn man, and her pleas meant nothing to me.

This was how it had to be.

She turned her face into my shoulder and let her tears drip onto my t-shirt. Tears or no tears, she was stunning. When she gripped my body and clung to me for comfort, it was so sexy. It made me want to have the driver pull over on the side of the road so I could take her in the back seat.

I might actually do it if I weren't thinking about my own death.

At least it would be painless. The lights would be out instantly, and the suffering would be over.

Best way to go.

The car pulled up to the restaurant. It belonged to a mutual friend and had been closed down for the day. It would just be the two of us with a couple of our men. No need for weapons and armies. Only one of us was walking out of there alive.

The back door was opened, but Arwen squeezed me harder so I couldn't get out.

I turned my gaze back to her and let her hold on to me. "You've got to be strong in there, alright? He feeds off fear. He wants to see you scared. He wants to see you cry." My thumb streaked across her cheek and wiped away the last drop of moisture. She hadn't put on any eye makeup, so there wasn't a mess left behind. "Keep it together."

"How could anyone keep it together?"

I squeezed her hand before I let go. "You will." I stepped out of the car, and she followed behind me. We entered the empty restaurant and found Kamikaze sitting at one of the tables in the center of the room. It was a table for six—and he sat right in the middle. Facing me with a glint of joy in his eyes, he grinned and showed all of his teeth. A gun sat on the table, the gun that would kill one of us.

Arwen sucked a deep breath when she laid eyes on him. It was the first time she'd seen him since he'd assaulted her, and even though she'd had a day to prepare for this meeting, that wasn't enough.

I walked in first, my four men moving with me.

Kamikaze stretched out his hand and gestured to the seat across from him. "Not a bad night to get shot in the head." The blinds were closed on all the windows, so the interior of the restaurant was invisible to the public. Little bottles of olive oil were on the tables, along with tablecloths and silverware. Paintings hung on the walls, and while there were no cooks in the kitchen, it still smelled like freshly prepared pasta.

My men pulled out the chair for me so I could sit across from him. "It's not a bad night for *you* to get shot in the head."

He grinned at my comeback. "We'll see in just a few short minutes." He turned his head and shifted his expression to Arwen, who was standing behind me in the corner. His eyes took her in, the arousal entering his gaze the second he looked at her. Just like all her other admirers, he eye-fucked her right in front of me.

"Don't look at her."

His eyes shifted back to me.

"She's still mine until that bullet fires off." I wouldn't have him gawk at her the entire time, claiming her before he had any right to.

His grin fell away, but he did as I asked. "Anything you want to say before we get started?"

"I'm not much of a talker."

He chuckled. "Neither am I. That's why I've always liked you." He gestured to the gun, signaling for his men to follow his orders.

One of the guys grabbed the gun in the center of the table then opened the barrel. He showed it to both of us—proving that it was empty.

I nodded.

Kamikaze did the same.

He grabbed a single bullet from his pocket and dropped it in a single slot. His thumb clicked in the barrel then he gave it a hard spin, making the bullet cycle into a random position. The gun was placed on the table once again, between the two of us.

Staring at the gun forced me to accept reality. This was happening. On the first go, I had a one-in-six chance of blowing my brains out. With every turn, the odds got higher and higher...until one of us finally croaked.

Kamikaze snapped his fingers. "Can we get some drinks over here? We'll both take a scotch—neat."

The guys scrambled around until the glasses were placed in front of us.

Arwen stayed in the corner, her muffled tears slightly audible. She sniffled occasionally, doing her best to stay strong but failing miserably. Good thing Kamikaze respected my wishes and kept his gaze on me.

"Coin toss?" He brought the glass to his lips and took a drink.

I gave a slight nod.

The same guy who handled the gun pulled a euro out of his pocket. He held it up for both of us to see, then he placed it on his thumb. "Call it in the air." He released his finger and launched the coin to the ceiling.

I kept my gaze locked on his as I heard the coin flip into the air.

Kamikaze made the call before it landed back in his palm. "Heads, he goes first."

Going first gave the best chance of survival because the odds of not getting the bullet were the greatest. But regardless of who went first, they were still shitty odds.

The man caught the quarter and looked at the landing. "Heads."

Arwen sucked in a deep breath through her teeth.

I didn't blink an eye over it. I still had a chance to survive this.

Kamikaze smiled like he disagreed.

I brought my glass to my lips and took a long drink before I reached for the gun. Silver and heavy, it was an antique. It was the kind of weapon used for special occasions like this, not in open combat. It was far too valuable to use on a random person. This gun was meant to give a dignified death.

I examined the weapon and felt the heft in my hand before I pointed it at my temple.

"Oh my god." Arwen immediately lost her cool. She started to hyperventilate and sob. "No…"

Kamikaze kept his eyes on me.

My finger hugged the trigger, and I looked into the eyes of my enemy, feeling my heart rate pick up slightly when I understood I could die in the next few seconds. I would squeeze the trigger—and either live or die.

Kamikaze held up his glass, like he was making a toast.

My fingers tightened on the trigger, but I didn't pull it just yet. I could hear Arwen struggling in the corner, her tears throbbing out of her throat. I wanted us both to walk out of there alive. But just because I wanted that, didn't mean it would happen.

Squeeze.

The gun clicked, but the bullet never came.

Arwen sucked in another deep breath, her cries still audible.

I set the gun in the middle of the table and grabbed my scotch again.

Kamikaze snatched the gun, pointed it at his temple, grinned like a psychopath, and then pulled the trigger—in less than a couple of seconds. Like a man with a death wish, he didn't take the time to savor the scotch on his tongue, the air in his lungs. He was such a maniac that there was no need to pause. It actually gave him a high.

He slid the gun back toward me. "We're at fifty-fifty, Maverick."

The gun sat in front of me, the silver weapon looking more intimidating now that my odds had just decreased significantly. This was the third try, which meant I had a twenty-five percent chance of getting the bullet.

I didn't like those odds.

Arwen became louder, not bothering to try to be quiet anymore. Her distress was like a car alarm in the middle of the night.

I picked up the gun and pointed it at my head.

Now I didn't feel so good about this.

"No...please." Arwen abandoned her attempt at being strong. She was coming apart with every second—and I couldn't help her.

I had to win—but I had no control over that.

Kamikaze swirled his glass before he took a drink. "What are you waiting for, Maverick?"

My finger wrapped around the trigger, and I kept my hand steady. It didn't matter how fearless a man was. When an enemy shot you in the head, you held your head high until the end. But to pull the trigger on yourself...that took a whole new level of courage. It went against biological nature to kill yourself so brutally. But I had to pull the trigger—no matter what happened.

Squeeze.

"Stop..." Arwen slid down to the floor, openly weeping in both terror and relief.

I pushed the gun toward him. My reaction was still stoic, but my heart relaxed now that the threat was over. Hopefully, he got the bullet on this round. He would be dead, and all my problems would be solved.

If only I were that lucky.

Even though he had a sixty-six percent chance of blowing his brains out, he moved with the same quickness as before. He pointed the barrel right into his temple and squeezed the trigger.

The gun clicked with the empty chamber.

Shit.

"No...please." Arwen rushed to the table and started to plead with Kamikaze. "I'll come with you, okay? I surrender. Just let him walk away—"

"Sit the fuck down." I refused to look at her. This was between the two of us—and she shouldn't have interfered. "Now."

Kamikaze didn't look at her either.

Arwen gripped my shoulder. "Please...please take me with you."

I pushed her off. "Don't make me ask you again."

Kamikaze waited for me to pick up the gun.

One of my men grabbed Arwen and dragged her away.

I picked up the gun, its weight more noticeable in my grasp. It seemed to get heavier with every turn, like the bullet inside with turning from lead to stone. My hand didn't shake even though there was a slight tremor in my fingertips.

Arwen screamed from her position against the wall. The men kept her pinned down so she couldn't rush me again. She didn't understand that Kamikaze wouldn't take her deal even if he wanted to. He was committed to this—and he had to see it through.

It was the first time Kamikaze dropped his indifferent attitude. His hands came together in front of his mouth as he stared at me, wishing that bullet to be inside the chamber. If the bullet didn't pierce my skull, then we knew the outcome of the match.

This turn was just as important as the last.

"Maverick..." Arwen said my name through her tears, a complete mess in the corner.

I tuned out her hysterics and held the gun steady against my temple.

Kamikaze didn't crack a smile or taunt me. He held his breath as he waited for me to decide our fates.

In just a second, I would be dead—or I would be the victor.

My blood ran ice cold, but sweat started to mark my forehead. If I died tonight, my life would have been short-lived. I would die a young man, following my mother into the afterlife. My sister would probably kill herself, and my father would be alone—until he put a bullet in his own brain.

My finger steadied on the trigger.

Squeeze.

My eyes closed as I heard the click of the barrel.

Instead of me dropping to the ground dead, everything went quiet as silence ensued. Then the slight sounds picked up again, like my own breathing and Arwen's sobs. Everything grew louder, reminding me I was truly alive.

I opened my eyes and looked into his.

He lowered his hands to the table, taking his loss like he didn't feel anything. His hard expression didn't change. His smile wasn't forthcoming, and he didn't break the tension with an inappropriate joke.

I set the gun in the center of the table.

Kamikaze stared at it for a long time, his eyes soaking in the sight of his own murder weapon. He wouldn't survive another bullet to the brain. This would kill him.

Even though Arwen knew I would live, she cried even harder.

I didn't like this man and shouldn't pity him. He'd hardly been an ally to begin with, but he was never an enemy before. He'd tried to rape my wife and sell her like a mule. But it was still depressing watching a man grappling to accept his own death. "I'll make a deal with you. Drop this for good, and we'll forget the whole thing." Kamikaze could be useful in the future. He owed me his life, so if I ever needed a favor, he would make it happen.

Kamikaze stared at the gun for a few more seconds before he lifted his gaze to meet mine.

"Just don't come near my wife again, and we have a deal." It was a generous offer, and he'd be stupid not to take it.

"And be your bitch for the rest of my life?"

"I wouldn't put it like that."

He grabbed the gun and dragged it toward him. "We made a deal—and I'll keep my end of the bargain." He brought the barrel to his forehead. "I wouldn't have given you the same mercy."

"You don't have to—"

Squeeze.

The gunshot went off, loud in the small enclosure of the restaurant. Drops of blood sprayed everywhere, covering the other chairs and the table in between us. His heavy body jolted with the momentum then crumpled to the ground with a loud thud.

His men stood their ground and did nothing.

I stared at the spot where he'd been. A terrifying man had just met my gaze, and then, instantly, he was gone. It reminded me of my mother in the strangest way...the fact that she was there one moment then gone the next. Life was fleeting and could be snuffed out within the snap of a finger.

Arwen rushed to me and wrapped me in her arms. Her face moved into my neck, and she held on to me like she needed the support to stand even though I was the one who'd almost died. She squeezed me tightly then cried into my ear, sobbing for so many reasons.

I was still numb from the transaction, still pumped with adrenaline that overwhelmed my system. My mind wasn't as sharp as it was because I was in a fog, still recovering from the near-death experience. That could be me lying on the floor, bleeding out everywhere.

But somehow, it wasn't.

## 17

## ARWEN

Maverick was the one who almost died.

But I was the mess.

The second Maverick stepped away from Kamikaze's dead body, I launched myself into his arms and sobbed into his chest. I already forgave him for pushing me away, for talking down to me like I was a dog that didn't know how to heel. I was just so relieved he was okay, that the bullet had been meant for his opponent instead.

Now that Kamikaze was dead, Maverick's arm wrapped around my waist, and he cupped the back of my head. He brought me close to him and let me cry into his chest, supporting me as I combated the horrific sight I just witnessed.

I watched a man shoot himself in the head.

I didn't care about that. I only cared about the man who was still standing.

"I'm alright, Sheep." He rested his lips against my temple,

becoming the affectionate man I remembered. Now that the threat was over, he dropped his hard-core attitude and returned to the sensitive man who shared my bed.

"I was so scared..." I'd never been so terrified in my life. When I thought that bullet might be for Maverick, I'd thrown myself at Kamikaze and prayed he would take me. I gladly would have gotten on my knees and did anything he asked to spare Maverick's life.

"I know." One of his men came to him and handed over the silver gun.

Maverick eyed it before slipping it into the back of his jeans.

"You're going to keep it...?"

"It's tradition."

---

Maverick sat in the back seat with me, his arms around me as I continued to process the trauma I'd just witnessed. My body wouldn't stop shaking with fear even though Maverick was with me now. The fact that he had to go through it at all was still troubling.

But now, Kamikaze was dead.

There was no one who wanted to kill me anymore.

My husband saved me. He'd calmly put that gun to his temple and pulled the trigger over and over. "You were so brave..." When Kamikaze had cornered me in the alleyway, I fought against him, but I also panicked. I didn't keep the calm composure Maverick did. I was fucking terrified.

His chin rested on my head, and he looked out the window as the landscape passed by. The afternoon had faded to night quickly as fall deepened. Lights from the passing houses became brighter in contrast.

I hugged his waist and relied on him as my crutch like I always did. This man married me because he had to, but now he protected me because he wanted to. He was willing to lay down his life for mine just to keep me safe.

How did I get so lucky?

We returned to the house and walked inside like it was an ordinary evening. My arm hooked through his as we walked into the house. I wasn't this affectionate on a daily basis, but almost losing him made me value him even more.

The smell of dinner was noticeable from the kitchen.

Abigail came out, wearing a black apron with a spot of sauce on the tip of her nose. She wasn't smiley like usual, looking at Maverick like he was a friend rather than her employer. Her eyes took him in, like she wanted to see his face herself. "You're back…"

Maverick stepped away from me and gently placed his hand on her shoulder. Wordlessly, he gave her a squeeze to acknowledge her feelings. He dropped his embrace then turned away.

Abigail's eyes watered as she watched him walk away, affection so bright in her eyes, it was impossible to miss. "Dinner will be served shortly." She smoothed out her apron then turned around to walk back into the kitchen.

I followed Maverick into the dining room and watched him pour himself a glass of wine as if everything was normal, as if he hadn't just watched a man shoot himself in the head. He poured a glass for me as well before he set the bottle down.

I sat across from him—numb. "She loves you…"

"Of course she does. I'm her boss."

"I don't think that has anything to do with it." That woman loved him like family. It wasn't a sibling kind of love or a romantic one. It wasn't even motherly. It was just love in its purest form.

He took a drink then licked his lips. "I'm starving."

The sight of blood had killed my appetite. "I don't see how you could be…"

His fingers rested on his wineglass as he stared at me across the table. He was oddly calm about the whole thing, just as indifferent as he was before we left. He swirled his wine then set the glass on the table again. "It's over. Time to move on."

"But you could have died—"

"But I didn't. Everything worked out. Kamikaze is gone."

All I should feel was grateful in that moment, but I was still shaken up about the entire thing. It would take me weeks to get over it. It was the most gruesome thing I'd ever seen. I would rather be raped a million times than let Maverick shoot a bullet into his own skull. "You were so calm… Did you think you weren't going to get the bullet?"

"No."

"So, you thought you were?"

"On my last round, I didn't know what was going to happen."

And he still acted totally normal? That was a sign of strength I'd never seen in my life. "How could you feel the cold metal of the barrel against your temple without panicking? How could you experience that moment without drowning in terror?"

He drank his wine again. "There are worse things than death."

"But not many things..."

"I don't want to talk about this anymore." Abigail came into the room with the hot dish and set it in the center of the table with two serving spoons. She also brought a salad and a basket of fresh bread. She looked at Maverick the same way she had just a moment ago, like she was so happy he was home. She excused herself quietly then left the room.

I watched Maverick dish the food onto his plate, pretending this was a normal night. He brushed off the event like it wasn't traumatizing, like it was something everyone experienced at some point in their lives.

I wasn't hungry, and I wasn't in the mood to pretend nothing happened.

I rose from my chair and felt his gaze move to my face. "I'm going to bed." I left my glass of wine behind and turned my back to him, letting him eat alone. I wasn't ungrateful for what he did for me, but I wasn't in the mood to pretend I hadn't almost just lost my husband. The evening was emotional for me. I'd lost both of my parents, and now Maverick was all I had left.

What would I do without him?

---

I stood in the shower and let the warm water soften my stiff muscles. Strands of my wet hair stuck to the back of my neck, and I entertained myself by watching the rivers of water run down the tile to the drain below my feet. Blood felt caked onto my skin, stuffed under my fingernails. I needed to get clean, needed to wash away the guilt I felt in my stomach.

Maverick almost died because of me.

I admired him for being so strong and dignified about the whole thing. I used to be that way, logical and pragmatic about all situations in life. But now I was an emotional woman who became distraught over her husband's well-being. I shed tears so quickly, and my heart was always on the verge of collapsing. Life was so much easier when I didn't care about anything. But now I cared so much about that man.

I cared about him more than anything else in this world.

He changed me in so many ways…and not necessarily for the better.

Distracted by my thoughts and the warm water, I didn't notice Maverick entering the shower until the door clicked behind him.

I pulled my hair over one shoulder then turned to look at him, seeing his fit body and tanned skin. His old bullet wounds were noticeable because they contrasted against his perfect skin…but they also made him more beautiful. Those scars were a part of who he was, the battles he'd won and lost.

The indifference finally disappeared from his gaze, and he looked at me with the affection I craved. He came up behind me and wrapped his arms around my waist. His warm chest pressed into my back, and he tightened his arms against my stomach.

I let him tug me into him, let myself fall back into his hold.

His lips placed a soft kiss against my neck. Another one was placed behind my ear. He bent his neck down to get my shoulder, to give me a kiss with a subtle bite.

I closed my eyes and got swept away in his embrace.

His hard cock pressed into my back, and he draped his arm over my chest so he could keep me in place. Then his kisses turned more aggressive, the edge of his teeth slightly scratching me as he kissed me harder and harder.

The water ran down us both as he kissed me like an animal, kissed me like a wolf claiming his mate. He pulled me harder against him and kept going, kissing me like he never had before. He kept tugging on me even though I couldn't get any closer. He grabbed my hips and pulled forcefully, wanting me to feel just how hard he was.

His mouth moved to my other shoulder, and he claimed the skin just like on the other side. His lips sucked my skin, and his tongue tasted the drops of water from the shower. When his mouth moved behind my ear, his hot breaths were audible over the falling water. His breaths sounded like growls, and his fingers started to feel like claws.

I closed my eyes and let him have me, let him take me however he wanted.

---

OUR WET BODIES lay on the bed, the moisture soaking into the duvet and the sheets. My wet hair immediately drenched the pillows underneath my head. My thighs were guided open by his knees, and his large body positioned itself over me. His narrow hips fit between my thighs, and his thick arms locked behind my knees. He held himself on top of me, supporting most of his weight on his arms like the exertion was so easy for him.

His mouth lowered onto mine, and he kissed me the way he did in the shower, so possessively. His took my mouth and claimed it as his, his hungry lips sucking and kissing mine. His tongue reached inside my mouth and danced erotically with mine, making my pussy just as wet as the rest of my body.

I'd given myself to him because he was the only man I wanted. This man was my husband, and he owned me—and I wanted him to own me. There was only one man I wanted to fuck me, to have me every single night in the same bed. He turned me on like crazy, making me a volcano that could erupt at any moment. He made my other lovers seem like a childhood phase. I thought I could have loved Dante, but being with Maverick made me realize how wrong I was.

He rested his lips against mine as he guided his length to my entrance. His thick crown pushed inside my eager lips, getting through the tight tunnel before he slowly sank the rest of the way.

My nails dug into his muscular arms, and I moaned.

He moaned too.

Slowly, he sank deeper and deeper inside me, gliding until our bodies were perfectly connected together.

God...that felt right.

He held my gaze for a few seconds as he felt me, as his cock absorbed the slickness that lined my channel from beginning to end. The grooves of his dick were so easy to feel because he was thick like a tree trunk. Feeling his balls against my entrance just made the pleasure better. He had me pinned underneath him, taking a moment to embrace the connection of our bodies.

My fingers moved into his wet hair as I felt how much he stretched me. We'd been together so many times, but it never had felt this good. It never had felt this intimate, this beautiful. Skin-to-skin and heart-to-heart, we were connected as deeply as two people could possibly be.

It felt so damn good.

I breathed hard in his face, little moans coming from deep in my throat. My fingers cradled his cheeks and I kissed him, so full with his fat dick inside me. He was all man, from his length to his width. It felt like the first time...like a wedding night.

I brought his lips to mine and kissed him. It was sensory overload, the way he felt between my legs and the way his dick felt inside me. He'd turned me on so much in the shower, the way he possessed me like a wolf possessed his sheep. I'd turned to melted butter long before we got to the bed.

His sexy lips moved with mine, and he started to rock into me, sliding his enormous dick through my slick pussy. He moaned as he felt me, moaned as his length pushed through my tightness over and over.

My husband was inside me for just a few seconds before I released. The heat entered my entire body, making it shake like an earthquake. My thighs stayed apart because of his arms, and by the time the sensation hit my pussy, I writhed on the bed. My fingers gripped his hair, and I stopped kissing him so I could enjoy the best climax of my life. Stuffed full of his cock and wrapped in his protection and devotion, it was heaven. "Maverick..." I opened my eyes and looked into his as it hit me so hard. "Yes..." I watched his eyes darken as he watched me. He made me come the second he was inside me because I'd been so eager for him...so eager for my husband.

He kept his pace slow so he could watch me enjoy him. He studied my reactions, watching the way my eyes filled with tears as I surrounded his dick with my come. He watched my mouth widen into a scream. His hips worked slowly to thrust inside me, to slide through the cream I produced just for him.

When I finished, I brought his face close to mine and held on to him. "I want your come inside me..." I grabbed his ass and directed his thrusts deep inside me, wanting him to explode with his eyes locked on mine.

His cock was so thick, it started to hurt. He crushed his body to mine, his hard stomach grinding against my pelvic bone. Without increasing his pace, he hit me deeper and deeper, his entire body tightening as he prepared for the goodness that would make him shudder.

My nails cut into his skin, and my pussy tightened in preparation for the seed he was about to give me. I wanted to take my husband's come, feel his satisfaction inside me. "Come on…"

He rested his forehead against mine as he gave his final pumps, his hips moving a little quicker as he shoved himself inside me. When he hit his trigger, his entire body tightened, and he closed his eyes as he succumbed to the climax. A sexy groan escaped his throat as he shuddered, his cock releasing inside me. He pumped me full of his come, the heavy substance so warm.

It was everything I had fantasized it would be, the kind of pleasure that made my toes curl until they cramped. My hands gripped his back, and I brought him close to me, his cock still hard inside me. "Again."

---

MAVERICK RESUMED his life like nothing had changed.

He got up early, worked out, and had breakfast before heading to work. He stayed at the office most of the day then drove into the city to meet with clients. He was closed off and a little cold during the day, but when he came to bed, he was the aggressive wolf that kept the sheets warm.

I drove to the factory on the other side the property and found him sitting at his desk in his office. His laptop was there, along with piles of paperwork and an empty ashtray. He sat in the leather chair and looked out the window, enjoying the sight of the house in the distance. From this angle, he could see the road that led to the factory, so he probably saw my car as I approached.

He didn't turn around to look at me.

He could pretend that night didn't affect him, but it clearly did. It still left noticeable scars in his eyes, a trauma that he couldn't easily forget. Even though Kamikaze threatened me and he was a horrible man, Maverick hadn't been eager to kill him. He was willing to sacrifice his life for mine, but he wasn't bloodthirsty like most men.

I leaned against the doorframe and stared at him.

His chin was propped on his fingertips as he examined his property. With the cooler weather, he wore dark blazers over his t-shirts and traded his shoes for boots. He'd gotten a haircut recently, so it directed more attention to his handsome face. He was a beautiful man…and he was mine.

I stepped farther into the room and rested my fingertips against the mahogany wood. The picture frame I gave him for his birthday sat there. His pretty mother smiled at the camera as she posed with her son. It was one of the rare times I could actually see Maverick smile rather than pout. I picked up the frame and looked it before setting it down again.

He still didn't look at me.

He always seemed to be in a mood. "What's bothering you?"

"Why do you assume that something is?"

"Because I know you."

He finally dropped his propped elbow and gave me his full focus. His eyes looked like steaming coffee, and his lips looked kissable. Whenever they devoured my naked body, they were so aggressive. He ate my pussy just as hard as he ate my mouth. He stared at me with that dark look.

"There's always something bothering you."

He smiled slightly, finding that truth comical. "True."

"So, what is it this time?" I came around the desk and leaned against the hard wood. With my arms crossed over my chest and the window in front of me, I waited for his tale.

He turned his gaze out the window once more.

"Is it Kamikaze?"

He shook his head slightly. "I don't care about that."

"Then what's on your mind?"

He didn't blink, his eyes taking in the landscape. "I called my father before it happened. Told him what Kamikaze and I were about to do. He didn't say much…"

He didn't need to give me the details to convey his pain. Even with Maverick on the verge of death, his father didn't care about him. That man was so cold that I didn't understand how his blood hadn't frozen over.

"And he hasn't contacted me since. He probably heard the outcome of the matchup at some point, but still…I expected something." Maverick wore the same stoic expression whether he was angry or solemn. He hid his emotions well because his eyes never gave him away. But I could see the subtleties in his shoulders and arms. I could see it in the way he carried himself, the way his eyes slightly shifted downward. "All of this happened because my mother died. Sometimes I wonder where I would be if she hadn't. Would my family still be together? But then it makes me question that relationship altogether. If it was only good when things were good...was it ever real?"

It should be the same through the good and the bad, but I felt that was an unnecessary statement to make.

"It makes me wonder if he ever wanted kids. My mother must have forced him. Now that she's dead, he wants nothing to do with us. You'd think I just get over it and move on with my life...but it still bothers me." Maverick was vulnerable with me without shame. He wore his heart on his sleeve and showed his true colors. He'd slowly allowed me inside his heart and his mind. Our partnership grew stronger, and our marriage became more real. It really felt like we were a man and a woman devoted to each other, there for each other always.

I moved to his chair and sat in his lap. My arm wrapped around his shoulders, and I rested my head against his. Blanketing him with empty words wouldn't make him feel better, especially when I had nothing substantial to say. It would be easy to lie and say his father loved him...deep down. But I couldn't say that unless I actually believed it to be true. Saying nothing at all was all I could offer him.

His arm wrapped around my waist as his head rested on my chest.

"I may not be the DeVille you want...but I'm still a DeVille. And we'll make our own family someday."

## 18

## MAVERICK

When Arwen entered the bedroom, she spotted the gown hanging from the bedpost. Champagne pink with a plunging neckline in front, it was sexy but also classy. My shopper picked it out for her and assured me it would be the perfect dress.

When her eyes almost turned into heart shapes, I knew she had been right.

Arwen walked up to the dress and touched the fabric with her fingertips. "Oh my god…please tell me this is for me."

"You better not think it's for me."

She ran her fingers down the fabric before she picked it up and held it against her frame. "I can tell it's going to look great. When is the party?"

"Tonight."

"You never give me much notice, huh?"

I shrugged then continued to look through my mail at the table.

She carried the dress to the full-length mirror and held it up to her body as she examined it. "So, what's the party for?"

"One of my clients is having a celebration."

"A celebration of what?"

"I don't know. Being rich?"

She turned to me. "You never throw parties."

"Because I don't need to blow up my ego." It was big enough already.

"Do you think they'll ask me to sing?"

"No. They'll expect it." After I finished looking through the mail, I turned to look at her. I watched her stare at the dress with loving eyes, falling in love with it right on the spot. When she smiled like that, her beauty was unparalleled. I watched her for a moment longer before she caught my look in the reflection. "Is that okay?"

"It's fine. I have a new song anyway. I think they'll like it."

"They'll like anything that you sing as long as you wear a low-cut dress."

She rolled her eyes but smiled at the same time. "Thank you for the dress. I love it." She walked over to me and rose onto her tiptoes to kiss me on the lips. It was an ordinary kiss, but it was packed with so much affection, a quick touch from a grateful wife to her husband. She lowered herself back to the floor and walked away.

My eyes followed her, my chest filled with a warmth

that could melt chocolate. Seeing her eyes lit up like that made my mouth want to smile. Giving her gifts she loved made me feel valued. Making her happy made me happy. When I put that gun to my head and pulled the trigger, I was doing it for her—and it felt right.

Just six months ago, we hated each other.

But now…everything was different.

She went to the dresser and found the black jewelry box sitting there. "Ooh…is this for me too?"

"I want you to wear it tonight."

She cracked the box and found a pair of diamond earrings sitting inside. She had more jewelry than she knew what to do with it, but she found each piece special. She immediately took them out of the box and slid them into her earlobes before she checked her appearance in the mirror. "They're beautiful. They'll look perfect with this dress." She turned back around, still beaming. "Thank you for spoiling me."

"You're my wife…you should be spoiled."

---

WE PULLED up to the luxurious three-story estate, and the valets opened the doors for us.

Arwen whistled under her breath. "Talk about fancy…"

I gave her a hand and helped her to her feet. She wore sky-high heels, the kind that didn't even allow the arch in her foot to touch the bottom of the shoe. I supported her as she righted herself and stood up straight. "It's been in the family for generations."

"You only socialize with super-rich people?"

"What other kind of people are there to socialize with?" I took her hand in mine and guided her past the water fountain and toward the entryway of the large home.

"Uh, normal people."

"Normal people are boring." I looked down at her, seeing her diamond necklace around her neck and the perfect way she'd applied her makeup. Before I even walked inside, I knew my wife would be the most beautiful woman there. She stole the show every single time—even when she wasn't in the theater.

"Why don't you have a party at your place?"

"I don't like people."

She chuckled. "You like me."

I brought her in closer to my side. "Don't let that go to your head."

She smiled then hooked her arm through mine, her long lashes bringing out the color of her eyes. Now that Kamikaze was gone and she stopped thinking about that gun pointed to my head, she'd relaxed into a whole new person. She didn't look over her shoulder or hunch in fear. There were no more monsters waiting in the dark.

That meant she didn't need to stay married to me anymore —but she never mentioned it.

Neither did I.

I had a feeling we never would.

We entered the party, grabbed champagne, and talked with a few acquaintances. Some of them were people Arwen already knew, but most of them were associates she hadn't had a chance to talk to.

Nearly every man eye-fucked my wife.

I took it as a compliment.

Mingling lasted for hours as appetizers were carried around by waiters. Our glasses kept getting replaced, and the volume in the room rose as people became chattier. Women wore their best dresses, and men had donned their best suits.

These parties weren't so boring now that I had a wife.

She did most of the talking—even though she didn't even know these people.

Fine by me.

I was done with the champagne, so I left her behind to grab a scotch from the bar. I placed my order then felt someone approach me. The piercing gaze they directed at me was hostile. It was something I could sense.

I grabbed my drink and turned to look at the man who wanted to cause trouble.

It was my father.

He never left his house anymore unless it was to kill someone, so it was a surprise to see him at a social event that required a suit. The last time I saw him dressed that way was at my wedding. I took a drink as I looked at him, swallowing the booze as well as my damaged feelings. "Nice to see you get out, Caspian." I couldn't call him my father anymore. It was a name too intimate to use at this point. He was an enemy, not an ally. He was a stranger, not a friend. "Surprised to see me? Thought the bullet in the chamber would be for me?"

He kept the same stony expression on his face.

"Looks like I disappointed you…again." I needed to accept the difficult truth—my father hated me. It didn't matter how much I hoped otherwise. The truth was difficult to swallow, but I had to get it down my dry throat anyway. "I should get back to my wife now. Try anything, and I'll watch your brains splatter on the wall—just the way I did with Kamikaze." With my drink in hand, I left him by the bar and returned to the beautiful woman in the pink dress. She'd just said something to make her admirers laugh.

I came to her side and placed my arm around her waist.

She glanced down at my drink. "No more champagne?"

"Too sweet for me."

"You mean, it's not strong enough," she teased.

The group laughed again.

I shrugged in response.

Lydia, one of the wives of my associates, addressed the one topic I didn't want to discuss. "I saw your father is here this evening. Seems to be getting better after losing your mother. How's he doing?"

Arwen immediately dropped her smile.

I wanted to tell the world that my father was a worthless asshole who should be dead instead of my mother. But I kept my mouth shut. "He's taking it one day at a time." After a few more exchanges, they walked away and left us alone together.

Arwen turned to me. "What did he say?"

"Nothing."

"Maverick," she pressed.

"No, he really said nothing. I blew him off at the bar then came back to you." I didn't turn back to where he'd been standing moments ago. I didn't want to acknowledge his existence at all. I wasn't the least bit scared of him or what he might do. "Don't worry about him."

She watched me with obvious concern. "You think he'll try to—"

"No." I brought her into my side and pressed a kiss to her temple. "Let's forget about him, alright?"

She nodded and went quiet.

Julian Levy stood up on a chair so everyone could see him across the room. He held up a glass of champagne then addressed the crowd. "Thanks for coming out, everyone. Nothing better than seeing happy faces swimming in champagne and bruschetta. I hope you all have a lovely evening." He raised his glass. "But we also have a special guest here tonight. I'm sure you all recognize her from her performance at the opera. Where is she?" He scanned the crowd and looked at Arwen.

"How are they not sick of me yet?" Arwen asked.

It wasn't surprising. I raised my glass in the air. "She's right here, Julian."

A blush entered her cheeks and nearly matched the color of her dress.

"Great," Julian said. "Can we borrow your wife for a song?"

I took the glass of champagne from her hand. "I know I can't hog her all the time."

Arwen looked at me with a hint of dread in her eyes, as if she still couldn't tolerate the idea of so many eyes on her. She won the affection of everyone in the room, like a magnet that attracted everything in its vicinity.

"Play that new song you told me about." I kissed her cheek before I let her go.

Arwen didn't want to walk away just yet. She still lingered beside me like that was the only place she really felt safe. After she gave herself a nudge, she finally walked away and pushed through the crowd until she reached the piano.

It was classic, black, and elegant.

I handed her glass to a waiter and waited for the music to begin. I was in the rear, but I was tall enough to see her easily. The high ceiling would still echo the music she played, so I would be able to hear it as clearly as if she were standing right beside me.

She smoothed out her dress and took a seat on the bench, her shoulders perfectly straight and her stomach tight. Her head tilted down toward the keys, a loose strand of hair falling with her movements. Her slender fingers gently landed on the keyboard, and she took a deep breath, like the magic was running through her fingertips at the touch.

This was the woman in my bed every night, the woman who made music every time she moaned for me. Her cries were ethereal, bringing a heavenly light into my previously dim home. When we met, she despised me and I despised her. But somehow, we brought out the best in each other. She made me more compassionate, and I taught her to shoot like a professional.

I took a drink as I waited for her to play, watched her struggle with her anxiety even though she knew she was a pro. Her voice could shatter crystal, and her fingers could create the most beautiful music in the world.

She finally started to play.

The sound of the piano filled the room, a tune that began slowly. Once she added her voice to the song, it instantly became a masterpiece. "Summer, bright as day. You took my hand and wiped my tears away. Leaving a past that haunts and stepping into a future so dark. I felt myself slip. I felt myself fall. But you caught me...after all." Her fingers danced across the keyboard faster as she headed into the chorus. "With arms that never let me go, a thumb perfect for the spilled tears, you're the man who completes me. The man who owns me. The man who loves me."

The crowd was silent as they watched her, affected by her music like it was a spell. The chitchat disappeared because her music was so enchanting. It splashed images in everyone's mind, added to the ambiance of the low-burning candles and flutes of champagne.

"When I lost my way, the meadow become so dark. Flowers

turned to thorns and winds turned to storms. Like a lone sheep, timid and afraid, I stood alone. Alone. Little did I know, he was always there. Warm coffee on a winter morning, his eyes like drops of chocolate. He was always there... even if I never knew." She didn't look up from the piano and became lost in the song, playing like she didn't know any of us were there at all. "With arms that never let me go, a thumb perfect for the spilled tears, you're the man who completes me. The man who owns me. The man who loves me."

Heads started to turn in the crowd, searching for my reaction. Several people had the same idea, so they all turned toward me.

She continued to play. "I can see the stars when he lifts me into the air. I can feel my fragile heartbeat when he comes near. My past is forgotten, buried in the ground. My maiden name is erased as he conquers. Cold sheets used to touch my chest, but now a deep heartbeat keeps the pace of my dreams."

More heads turned my way.

She went into the chorus one more. "With arms that never let me go, a thumb perfect for the spilled tears, you're the man who completes me. The man who owns me. The man who loves me. With a heart that will never let you go, lips perfect for yours, I'm the woman who completes you. I'm the woman who loves you." Her fingers hit a few more keys before the song ended. Silence filled the room, and now, most of the attention was directed at me.

I continued to stare straight ahead and refused to look at the ground. All eyes were on me, and I squeezed my glass a little tighter, uncomfortable with the unwanted attention.

People finally started to applaud for her, and the attention was taken off me.

I downed the rest of my scotch and set it on a passing tray.

Arwen stood up, and the applause grew louder.

I turned around and walked off, the cacophony of noise like nails against a chalkboard. The lights suddenly felt too bright, the collar around my neck too tight. I found the front door and stepped into the cold air, letting the sting of coming winter lower the heat the exploded in my blood.

The second the breeze touched my skin, I felt a little better.

But it wasn't enough.

## 19

## ARWEN

I spent the next hour taking questions about my music. The crowd surrounded me, and I didn't have an opportunity to find Maverick. I assumed he would come to my side, but he never showed up.

"That was a beautiful song." A woman I didn't even know rested her hand over her heart. "It takes me back to when Victor and I first got married. Maverick must have been very touched."

I hoped he was. "Thank you. Please excuse me." I parted the crowd and ignored people's questions as I searched for Maverick. He didn't seem to be anywhere in the main room, and since all the men wore black suits, he was difficult to spot. It was warm in there, so I decided to check outside.

There he was, drinking a glass of scotch while he let the nighttime air lick the sweat off his skin. He stood alone as he looked across the perfectly manicured lawn of the historic estate. The valet and other workers were there, but the rest of the guests were still inside.

I walked up to him, instantly cold once I wasn't in the protective bubble of heat the house provided. "There you are. It's hot in there, huh?"

"A bit." He finished the rest of his glass and handed it to a waiter as he passed. "Ready to go?"

He didn't compliment my performance. He didn't even look at me. Both hands were in his pockets now, so he had no intention of blanketing me with his usual affection. Just an hour ago, we were husband and wife. Now we were something akin to strangers. "Everything alright?"

"Yeah." He caught the valet's attention to retrieve the car.

The man took off at a run as Maverick walked toward the roundabout driveway with the large fountain in the center. He didn't take my hand and guide me down the stairs.

I followed behind him, feeling like a dog that got her nose slapped. "Why are you being like this?"

"Like what?"

"Well, for starters, you haven't looked at me."

The valet pulled up with the black Bugatti then tossed the keys to Maverick.

Maverick caught them. "I know what you look like." He opened the passenger door for me then moved to the other side.

I was so shocked by what he said that it took a second for me to move my feet and get inside the car.

Maverick drove off, driving far faster than necessary and speeding back to the house like he was racing against time.

I looked out the window, refusing to believe this was really happening. "I'm so disappointed in you... I thought we'd moved past this."

Maverick didn't acknowledge what I said. He kept his eyes on the road, both hands on the wheel even though he usually only drove with one. He didn't bother glancing in the rearview mirror and drove as fast as he could, wanting to get away from me as quickly as possible.

I wanted to slap him.

We returned to the house several awkward minutes later. We pulled into the garage then entered the house.

He was on a mission to get away from me. He didn't wait for me to catch up, even though my ridiculous heels made it impossible for me to match his stride. He entered the entryway and approached the stairs.

"Maverick."

He stopped on the bottom step but didn't turn around.

"You need to get over this bullshit. Be a man and buck up."

He slowly turned around, one hand resting in his pocket. It was the first time he'd really looked at me since I finished my song. Like we were back in time, he stared at me like he hated me. It was six months ago, and he despised having to welcome me into this house. "Get over what bullshit?"

"Your bullshit. This all goes back to your inability to accept affection, love, even a damn compliment. The second you get something, you pull away. Be a man and accept what I said. Be a bigger man and say it back."

His eyes shifted back and forth quickly as he looked at me, his body rigid with anger.

Was I stupid for assuming he was ready for this? Our feelings for each other were so obvious. Kamikaze was gone, and not once had he asked me to leave. I'd never tried to go either. We were together every night, ditching the condoms and making love as husband and wife. Did he really fail to grasp all of that? Hearing that someone loved him really scared him that much? "I'm not going to go away, Maverick. I'm not going to die, disappear, or turn my back on you." I wasn't going to become a thing of the past like his family. I was there to stay—forever. I was Mrs. DeVille, and I was staying that way. There was no one else I wanted to be with, and there was no one else he wanted to be with. We were together—until death parted us.

Without answering, Maverick turned around and walked up the stairs. His strong frame carried him to the second landing smoothly, and then he turned to take the steps up to his bedroom.

I stayed at the bottom in my pink dress, feeling abandoned and forgotten. That night started so beautifully, but then I expressed my feelings in the best song I've ever written, and it scared him.

I should be livid at his reaction.

Pussy.

But if he wanted to act that way, that was fine with me. He could take all the time he needed to sulk in his bedroom and brood while he was at the office. After he finished throwing his hissy fit, he would come to his senses and ask forgiveness.

And I would have a hell of a time making him earn it.

---

I STAYED in my room all day and didn't bother venturing to other parts of the house. Maverick would make sure he didn't cross my path. He would take his meals in his office and avoid me like the plague.

Asshole.

I was hurt that I'd put my feelings on display and he'd shot me down so coldly. Those lyrics came from my heart. They were real, and I didn't regret writing them down. I didn't regret composing that song.

I just wished Maverick would let go of his issues.

Losing the love of his family messed him up badly. His father was an ultimate asshole, so Maverick was incapable of accepting love, only insults. His shell had hardened so much that nothing could penetrate his exterior while his guard was up.

I thought his guard wasn't up around me.

I thought we were closer than that.

He could pretend he was incredulous about my feelings, but that was bullshit.

And he could pretend he didn't feel that too…but that was also bullshit.

In time, he would come to his senses. I just had to be patient.

I watched TV for most of the day then wrote music for the

second part of the afternoon. I was hurt by his reaction, so it was the perfect time to compose something raw, a deep catharsis. Loving a man incapable of love was quite the task to take on.

But I was willing to try.

When night deepened, my impatience started to get the best of me. We weren't boyfriend and girlfriend who lived separate lives in different places. We were husband and wife, two people with the same last name.

We shouldn't be acting like this.

He should be the bigger man and come to my bedroom. Even if he didn't want to talk, we should still be sleeping together. We should be screaming at each other but making love when it was all over.

Now that I had a husband I adored, that was exactly what I wanted to do…for the rest of my life.

I left my bedroom and headed down the hall to take the stairs. I knew Maverick felt the same way; he was just incapable of accepting love without any demands in return. He wasn't used to someone caring about him for him…and nothing else. Maybe I needed to be patient. Maybe I needed to hold his hand and get him through this. The man had put a gun to his forehead and pulled the trigger several times for me…of course he loved me.

I'd almost reached the staircase when I heard a woman laughing.

"No wonder why you're in such good shape if you walk up these stairs every day."

*The Wolf and His Wife*

I stopped in my tracks because it wasn't Abigail or one of the maids. She sounded trashy, like a dumb girl he'd just picked up at the bar. But that couldn't be true because Maverick would never do that to me.

Then I heard someone else. "I bet you could carry both of us up the stairs."

I heard Maverick's chuckle. It was deep, masculine, and sexy.

My heart fell into my stomach as my knees went weak. The ring on my left hand suddenly felt too tight, constricting the blood flow to all the body parts that needed it right now. I wanted to turn around and walk away, but I wanted Maverick to see my reaction, to let that look haunt him for the rest of his life.

He made it to the top of the stairs, a beautiful woman on each arm. "Your asses are gonna be a little plumper after this trip."

Both girls laughed because it was *so* funny.

My brain didn't react right away because it was sensory overload. My worst nightmare was looking me right in the face—and I didn't know it was my worst nightmare until it actually happened. Not once had we confirmed our commitment to each other, but it seemed so obvious that it didn't need to be said. We were together now…husband and wife. This felt like a betrayal.

It was infidelity.

Maverick turned the corner with the girls, not noticing me standing there.

I knew he wasn't trying to sneak around. He didn't care whether he got caught or not.

But I wanted him to know I was there. I wanted him to see the heartbreak in my eyes, to know he'd fucked this up permanently. "Maverick."

He stopped before the bottom step and barely turned his head to look at me. His arms stayed on the girls, like his allegiance was to him and not me.

Tears were hot in my throat, but I refused to let them rise to my eyes. If Maverick wanted to stoop this low, he wasn't worth my tears. If love made him do something stupid like this, then maybe I'd been wrong. Maybe what we had wasn't love.

Maybe it'd never been love.

He held my gaze, his brown eyes like two solid walls. He wasn't letting anything inside his emotional armor. I could be in tears right now, and he wouldn't give a damn.

That was why I saved my breath and didn't say a word. Nothing mattered in that moment.

He didn't care.

So why should I?

## 20

# MAVERICK

I SAT AT THE BREAKFAST TABLE WITH MY BLACK COFFEE IN front of me. Bags were under my eyes, and the remnants of sleep wouldn't leave the crevasses. I was exhausted from the long night, but it was impossible to keep sleeping. The two girls took up all the space in the bed, and they kicked me every few minutes.

I'd been with two women before. It was always a good time.

But I hadn't enjoyed myself.

I kept thinking about my wife.

She told the whole world she loved me and assumed I felt the same way. She humiliated me in front of a crowd of my peers and expected me to be touched by it. Our relationship suddenly shifted and became something else—something I wasn't ready for.

I never said I loved her.

If I felt that way, I would tell her.

My entire body shut down, and my walls shot up to the sky.

I didn't want what she wanted—and I made that abundantly clear.

But now I sat alone at the table, my coffee cold and my breakfast untouched.

The girls came down moments later and helped themselves to the food I would never eat. One was blond and one was brunette. Without trying to be polite, they grabbed whatever they wanted off the table and made a mess. They used the same knife in the butter as the jam, and they had no manners, so they were just obnoxious.

"So, what do you do?" the brunette asked before she bit into her toast and got crumbs all over the table. "Born rich?"

I stared at her and didn't bother responding. I just wanted the two girls out of my house. They wouldn't get another invitation to bed. Sleeping alone seemed preferable in hindsight.

Footsteps sounded on the stairs. Boots echoed against the wood, and the sound became louder as she drew near. Her pace was full of attitude, announcing her anger without the need for words.

I looked up and saw Arwen, a woman more beautiful than the two ordinary girls I'd slept with. She stared at me like I was nothing, a piece of gum on the bottom of her shoe. There was so much malice in her stare, like she hated me more than she'd ever hated Kamikaze. A stack of papers was in her hand, fresh white paper with a clip at the top. She pretended the girls didn't exist as she tossed the packet at me.

It landed in front of me and almost spilled my coffee.

I didn't look down to see what it was. I kept my eyes on her, noting the pain that existed underneath the rage. She shed her tears for me when she thought I might die, but they weren't forthcoming from this. She was too strong for that, way too damn stubborn.

With one hand propped on her hip, she stood in black jeans with a white top and leather jacket. She was dressed like she was ready to leave the house. Those blue eyes weren't so pretty anymore. They were cold as steel and malicious as blades. "I want a divorce." She let the words sink in for a moment before she turned around and walked off, her boots sounding against the hardwood floor once more. Her ass shook left to right as she stormed to the stairs and excused herself from the dining room.

I looked down at the papers she'd tossed at me. Her signature was at the bottom, and all she needed was for me to fill in the blanks. It looked legitimate. She must have called in a favor to someone to get this processed so quickly.

When I turned to the page that detailed her settlement in the divorce, I was surprised by what I saw.

She didn't want anything from me.

Not even a euro.

## ALSO BY PENELOPE SKY

My gravest mistake was falling in love with my husband.

It crept up on me so slowly that I didn't even notice it was happening until it arrived. I assumed he felt the same way every time he kissed me...every time he touched me.

Until he proved me wrong.

Kamikaze is dead, so I don't need him for protection anymore. Divorce is all I want now. I'll find a man that will love me the way I deserve, that won't bring home two strange women just to hurt me.

I don't need him.

Now it's time to start over.

Order Now

Printed in Great Britain
by Amazon